Kinds of Love,
Kinds of Death

Kinds of Love, Kinds of Death

Kinds of Death

A Mitchell Tobin Mystery

Donald Westlake

writing as Tucker Coe

Five Star
Unity, Maine

Five Star Mystery Series.
Published in 2000 in conjunction with Tekno Books
& Ed Gorman.

Set in 11 pt. Plantin by Al Chase.

Printed in the United States on permanent paper.

Library of Congress Cataloging-in-Publication Data

Coe, Tucker.
    Kinds of love, kinds of death / by Donald E. Westlake writing as Tucker Coe.
        p.   cm.
    ISBN 0-7862-2669-2 (hc : alk. paper)
    1. Tobin, Mitch (Fictitious character) — Fiction.
2. Private investigators — New York (State) — New York
— Fiction.   3. New York (N.Y.) — Fiction.   I. Title.
PS3573.E9 K56 2000
813'.54—dc21   00-030846

TO My Secret, *Love*

Introducing Tucker Coe

by Donald Westlake

The first few years I was writing, I produced far too much. If I'd been a little older I might have burned out, but as it was, I just kept finding new areas to explore, new ways to write, new subjects, new formats. I was like a kid who's just moved into a new neighborhood and won't be content until he's run through every new alley, climbed over every new fence, surveyed every inch of this new world.

All of that exuberance peaked in 1965, when I published twelve short stories, in magazines from *Playboy* to *Ellery Queen's Mystery Magazine*. The stories were all over the lot: mystery, science fiction, comedy, slices of life. In addition, Westlake wrote a novel, *The Spy in the Ointment* (I've always hated that title), and so did Richard Stark. But Stark, after eight novels about his character Parker, wrote *The Damsel*, his first novel without Parker, featuring Parker's associate Alan Grofield. And a new fellow, more short-lived, weighed in, one Curt Clark, with a science fiction novel, *Anarchaos*.

In addition to all that published work, I also scampered down some blind alleys, putting together two anthology ideas that nobody wanted, plus three movie treatments that nobody wanted (at that time, I still thought the word for those things was "outline") and two television series treatments that nobody wanted, one of which later became transmogrified into a novel of mine called *Help I'm Being Held Prisoner*.

The following year, 1966, at last I began to slow down, but at the same time I continued to expand. I wrote no short stories that year, no unwanted treatments, no unassembled anthologies (but one published anthology, my only, *Once Against the Law*, done with William Tenn). All I did that year was three novels, a Westlake (*God Save the Mark*), a Stark about Parker (*The Rare Coin Score*) and another brand-new guy, Tucker Coe.

In a way, Tucker Coe came out of my desire to unlearn something I'd perhaps learned a bit too well. When I was 14 or 15, I'd read *The Thin Man* (my first Hammett), and it was an astonishing read, I believe the single most important learning experience of my career. It was a sad, lonely, lost book, but it pretended to be cheerful and aware and full of good fellowship.

I hadn't known it was possible to do that, to seem to be saying one thing while you really said a different thing or even the opposite. It was three-dimensional writing, like three-dimensional chess, a writing style you could look through like water and glimpse the fish swimming by underneath. Nabokov was the other master of that, but Hammett I read first.

Much of the technique involved suffusing the story with emotions without mentioning the emotions. (Peter Rabe had that strength, too.) One way and another, I'd been trying to do something similar in my own early books and stories. Then, when comedy came in, that altered the situation, because comedy blankets emotion like radio interference. And Stark, of course, was poker-faced by definition. But wasn't it sometimes a good idea *not* to cloak the emotions? Was I letting one approach to story and character muffle me?

Tucker Coe came out of that. Mitch Tobin is a guy who's hurting so much, and so freshly, that he can't hide his emotions even though he desperately wants to. That was an interesting thing to try to do, write in such a way that the fish would break the surface sometimes.

Now, thirty-five years later, I can't remember how I came up with this particular character with this particular problem, but I do know I started out wanting to write a *mystery*, a story in which the hero solves a murder, or series of murders. Since I was never content to just ride the road already traveled, but always wanted to twist the concept or embellish it or alter it somehow, this time the idea was that the detective was reluctant to *be* a detective, because he had serious problems of his own that consumed all his attention. (I realize now, somewhat after the fact, that even in this I was echoing *The Thin Man*, in which Nick Charles is extremely reluctant to think about the disappearance of Clyde Wynant, having to be repeatedly prodded and nagged by Nora to get on with it.)

I liked Mitch Tobin, and I learned from him, but I'm afraid his end was in his beginning. The whole point with him was that the hurt was fresh. Over the next six years, I wrote a total of five novels about Mitch Tobin, but partway through the last of them, *Don't Lie to Me*, I realized I wouldn't be able to write about him any more, not after that book. Emotional wounds heal, or they fester and turn rank. Mitch had to get over his trauma one way or another. If he finally accepted himself so he could move on with his life, he'd be just another private eye, and no longer of interest to me. If on the other hand he became neurotic, stuck in the past, he might be interesting to psychiatrists, but not to me. I didn't kill him off, I didn't see any need to go that far, but at the end of that final book I let him sleep.

One last note, about the pen name. My first editor at Random House, through the sixties, was Lee Wright, known as the Queen of the mystery. A wonderful person and a fantastic editor, I learned a lot from her. She had little professional crotchets, however, such as refusing to let anybody use the word "dead" in a title (her only taboo word), so that the book I wanted to call *The Dead Nephew*, for instance, because I think the word "nephew" is comic, became called *The Fugitive Pigeon* instead, which is another title I've always hated. And never understood.

But that's a digression. Lee Wright's attitude toward pseudonyms was that the most memorable kind of moniker was a perfectly ordinary last name coupled with an unusual first name (Carter Brown, Cordwainer Smith, Marco Page). In the mid-sixties, I was a New York Giants football fan, and their running backs in those years were a couple guys named Ernie Koy and Tucker Fredericksen, so I said, "How about Tucker Koy?" Lee said, "I'm not sure why, but Tucker Koy sounds obscene." So he became Tucker Coe.

1

I was working on my wall when Wickler came around the side of the house and called, "Hey, Tobin, whatcha doin?" He had no right to use my name that way.

I put down my pick, stepped up out of the hole, walked over to him, turned him around, took him by the neck and butt, and double-timed him out to the street. "There's the front door," I said. "You want to see me, ring the bell."

"Christ!" he said, shooting his cuffs. "Christ!"

I brushed my hands and went back to my wall.

A wall is an important thing, a substantial thing, a thing worth a man's time and consideration. I was finding it possible to concentrate on this wall as I hadn't been able to concentrate on anything since . . . for six months . . . for a long while.

This was my third day of work on the wall. The first day I had designed it, with paper and pencil and ruler: two feet wide and ten feet high and completely enclosing the backyard, with no gates or openings, so people would only be able to get in here by going through the house. The second day I'd gone out and ordered the materials—concrete block and brick and cement—and then come back and laid out the position with sticks and string all the way around the yard. And now today I'd begun to dig.

If you're going to build a good wall, a wall to stand, then first you have to dig, because the wall should start down

11

inside the earth, down below the frost line. I figured in this climate two feet was deep enough, so I had a piece of one-by-three with a pencil line on it at two feet, and I was using it to check my depth as I went along. I also had a level, to be sure the bottom was even; at intervals I would lie my one-by-three on the bottom and set the level on top of it. With all this checking, and with my being somewhat soft and out of shape, the work was coming along slowly, but that was all right. I was in no hurry.

I'd done about seven feet so far, and had a hole two feet wide and two feet deep and seven feet long. When I came back to it from removing Wickler, I saw that it looked like a shallow grave, which I didn't like. I hopped down into it and grabbed my pick and began hacking away at the dirt again, in a hurry to make a hole too long to look like a grave. I didn't think about Wickler. I didn't think about anything.

A few minutes later Kate came out onto the back porch and called, "Mitch. Somebody to see you."

"In a minute," I said. "Put him in the den."

She stood watching me a few seconds and then went back into the house. I had no idea what she thought about the wall, and that was good. A wife should not have opinions about the way her husband breathes.

I was working with the shovel now, and I kept at it till I'd scooped all this last batch of loose earth up out of the hole. When I quit this time, it looked less like I was working on a grave. I stripped off my canvas gloves, dropped them on the ground beside the shovel, and went into the house.

Kate was in the kitchen, making a meatloaf. She's a raw-boned woman, and I've given her lines around the mouth and eyes she shouldn't have. She's thirty-five, four years younger than me, but whether she looks it or not I can't say; when you've been married to a woman sixteen years she looks neither old nor young but simply right.

"The store just called," she said. "They want me to come in, until nine."

I said, "You already worked two nights this week."

"We could use the money, Mitch," she said.

Was she thinking of the mounds of building materials in the backyard? I didn't know, and I didn't want to know.

There's a sullenness that comes with guilt that I'd never known until very recently. I'd always been a big one for speaking out, holding nothing in, but more and more these days I found myself turning away, mouth clenched, eyes lowered, chest filled with grim bile. Over the years most of the punks I'd arrested had had the same expression on their faces while being booked that I found these days habitually on my own.

Kate said, "I'll put the meatloaf in the oven before I go. I'll leave a note on the table."

I said, "All right," gracelessly, and went through the house and up the stairs to the second floor.

The den was what I called the smallest of the three bedrooms up there. Kate and I shared the largest, young Bill had the second, and the spare was to be my office away from the office. Another of my do-it-yourself projects, I'd started to make over the room ten years ago, when we'd bought this house. I'd laid thick carpet on the floor, soundproofed the ceiling, and put sheets of knotty pine paneling all around the walls, but that's as far as I'd gone. The built-in bookcases were still merely a stack of lumber leaning in one corner, and taped-over wires sticking out of the ceiling marked where I never put the light fixture in. But of course in those days I was busy, and full of activity, and pleased with life, and sometimes the unessential things didn't get done.

The only two pieces of furniture in the room were a battered desk and chair I'd taken from the precinct house seven years ago. Wickler, short and narrow and dressed like a race-track dandy, sat in the chair now smoking a thin cigar with a plastic tip.

I said, "Stand up."

He wanted to defy me because I wasn't on the force any longer, but he had sense enough to know I was a man aching to be pushed. After the slightest of hesitations he got to his feet and moved away to the left, giving me plenty of room to go past him and sit down.

I put my forearms on the desk. I felt small nerves jumping beneath the skin all over my body. I looked at my knuckles and said, "What do you want from me?"

"Ernie Rembek sent me," he said, and stopped as though that explained everything.

It didn't explain a thing. I'd already known that Wickler never moved anywhere but where Ernie Rembek sent him. I said, "What did he send you for?"

"He's got a job for you."

I said, "Be careful. Watch what you say."

He decided to be aggrieved. "You ain't on the force any more," he said, his voice squeaking. "Whatcha being so hardnosed about?"

I said, "You're not being careful."

"The hell with careful! You got kicked out, like any alley cat!"

I stood up and slapped him, backhand, not very hard. He fell back against the wall and leaned there, blinking at me. I said, "I never dealt with punks the whole time I was on the force. I was never on the take, not once, not for a penny. No one ever called me for dishonesty. I may have been kicked out, but it wasn't for being involved with scum like you. You go back and tell Rembek I'm the same man I always was. I never took a crooked job and I'm not going to start now."

He shook his head, holding his hand to the cheek I'd slapped. He said, "You got the wrong idea, Tobin."

"Mister Tobin."

He nodded. "Mister Tobin," he said. "It ain't the way you think. Ernie Rembek don't want you to do nothing crooked. He wants you to do a cop job. You used to be a cop, a good cop, and right now Ernie needs somebody to do a cop-type job."

"Not interested," I said. "I let you into the house for one reason, and this is it. To give you a message to bring back to Ernie Rembek. You tell him I am not interested in any deals, any offers, any propositions. Everybody's entitled to one mistake, even Rembek, so this time I do nothing but give you the warning. But he should send nobody else, not ever again."

"Mister Tobin," he said, "I swear to you I'm giving you straight goods. Nobody wants you to do nothing illegal, not even a little bit illegal. It's strictly a cop job Ernie wants done. Detecting, like."

"No," I said. I went over and opened the door.

"Lemme tell you the pay," he said.

"Time for you to leave," I told him.

But he stood his ground. "A flat five G for openers," he said. "Plus so much a day and expenses, you and him work it out together when you see him. Plus a bonus if the job works out okay."

"Wickler," I said, "it's time for you to leave."

He hung on a second longer, and I knew what he was thinking. Ernie Rembek had sent him to get me, and wouldn't be happy when Wickler went back to him empty-handed. But Rembek was a future threat, and I was a threat right in the room with him, so he hung on only for that one last second, and then he shrugged and said, "Okay, if you say so. But you can't say I didn't try."

"You tried," I gave him.

I had him precede me down the stairs, and past him I could see Kate in the front hallway, shrugging into her coat. "See you tonight," she called up the stairs to me. "I've got to run." She waved and went out the front door.

It seemed to me Wickler was going down the stairs too slowly. I was anxious to get back to my wall. The last few steps, I prodded his shoulder, muttering at him to shake it up. He trotted on down the rest of the way, saying something petulant, and I opened the front door for him.

It might still have been all right, if I hadn't seen her. But the angle out the door was just right and I did see her, walking away down the sidewalk, her coat flapping about her shins. I stepped out onto the stoop, crowding Wickler ahead of me, and shouted after her, "Kate! Take the *car!*"

"No, no," she called back, airy and effortless, "I feel like walking."

I knew what it was; she didn't want to use the gas. A backyard full of bricks and concrete block, and out front Kate was walking over a mile to a part-time job at a shopping center five-and-dime.

Wickler, like anyone unexpectedly present at a moment of domestic tension, was walking away along the path to the sidewalk, head down, affecting not to hear anything. Beyond him was the car. Off to the right, Kate had waved again and was walking on, walking quickly to be the sooner out of earshot.

In a flash, I thought of myself taking her place, showing up at the five-and-dime instead of her, standing at the long and crowded counter—

I could no more do that than I could answer a help-wanted ad in the Sunday paper. The thought of going for a job interview, the thought of that inevitable question about my previous employment, made my cheeks burn and my palms grow wet with nervous perspiration. And what can a man do today without going through that preliminary questionnaire? You can't even dig a ditch any more until you've answered all the questions and filled out all the forms.

I stood on the stoop, sweat cooling on my forehead, and watched Kate walk with quick strides on out of sight. Wickler had turned that way, too, but was moving more slowly, in no hurry to return empty-handed to his lord.

I called, "Wickler!"

I hadn't realized until then just how afraid of me the little hood was. He stopped in his tracks when I called his name, hunching his shoulders and ducking his head as though he expected to be pounded from behind at any second. Slowly, reluctantly, he turned to face me.

I'm not a hardnose by nature, it was only because of the last six months that I'd been so immediately hard with Wickler. I felt embarrassed at that now, and ashamed of myself, when I saw the effect I'd had on him. Trying to get more softness into my tone, I called to him, "Come on back here. Come here a minute."

He came, wary and reluctant, and as he moved toward me I had fresh doubts and second thoughts. But I could at least find out, I could at least do that much.

I said, as he stood below me, "This job. You say it doesn't break the law?"

"It doesn't even *bend* the law," he said, suddenly eager again. "I give you my word of honor, Mister Tobin, it's one-hundred-percent legit."

"All right," I said. "Come in and tell me about it."

This time I took him into the living room.

17

2

The past is the past. What I did to get myself kicked out of the New York Police Department has nothing to do with the story of Ernie Rembek and the "cop job" he wanted to hire me for, and it seems to me I would be well within my rights not to say a word about it. And yet I feel a compulsion to tell, to explain, even to justify. Or maybe just to confess. Or perhaps merely to play the masochist, and by bringing the story out again in words, to twist with my own hands the knife on which I've impaled myself.

I was a cop eighteen years, and in the course of the fourteenth year I had cause to make an arrest on a professional burglar named Daniel "Dink" Campbell. I made this arrest in Dink's home, an unprepossessing three-room apartment on the West Side of Manhattan. Violence was not Dink's style, so the arrest took place without incident, other than that in the process I first met Dink's wife, Linda Campbell, a short, pleasant-looking, ash-blond woman of twenty-eight, who accompanied her husband and me to the—

But the story tips itself right there, doesn't it? On first seeing Linda's name in print you know that I am destined to go to bed with her, knowledge that did not come to me until over a year later, when Dink had already been tried and convicted and was in the process of serving a term that at its shortest must last fifteen years. But it is impossible for me to communicate the knowledge to you as it came to me, in slow revelations, in tiny sunbursts of awareness, in gradual dependence and increasing need and a feeling that developed so slowly it was *there* long before either of us was fully aware of it, a feeling of *inevitability*. None of that rationalizing mist which so delightfully blinded me is available now to blind you; you must see it in a cold harsh light, a cheap and nasty bit of adultery with the most tasteless and degrading overtones. But that isn't how it seemed! (And how many bemused dreamers down the ages have cried that silly cry on awakening.)

Still, I cannot resist at least a bit of the rationalization. I have seen the wives of the yeggs, hundreds of them over the years, and they come to a pattern. Most frequently they are slatterns, slovenly frumps in disheveled apartments, as unintelligent and ill-educated and ambitionless as their pennyante husbands. The burglar, when his night's work is done, does not go home to the arms of a siren.

Not that Linda was a siren, by any means, but neither was she a slattern. A bright and vivacious woman, she had the usual insufficient New York City public school education, but had supplemented it in the years since with extensive reading, and in fact it was a common interest in the library that first brought us into awareness of one another.

I *won't* tell the whole story, all the stages, the reverses, the landmarks along the long slide down the endless easy slope into one another's arms. It happened. We had an affair that lasted three years.

It might have lasted more if nothing had happened outside us to stop it. But something did, and it stopped everything.

I could only see Linda while on duty, of course, all the rest of my time being too closely accounted for. This meant that one other person was in on the secret; my partner, Jock Sheehan. He covered for me and never said a word to me about what I was doing. In Jock's world, an adult was responsible for his own decisions. Jock helped me because he was my partner and my friend, not because he approved.

The arrest in which Jock was shot to death was one that should have been as easy as the arrest four years earlier of Dink Campbell. But it didn't work right; the numbers runner we were after had gone onto narcotics since we'd last been in touch with him. So we hadn't known that I should be along on that trip, and I wasn't along. Jock dropped me off at Linda's place, and went on to meet his death alone, and in his pocket was Linda's phone number in case he had to call me.

No one knew where I was. The first officers on the scene questioned witnesses, and no one had seen a second plain-clothes cop. Someone checked out that phone number, on the off-chance, and got the information from the telephone company, and happened to connect on the name Daniel Campbell—Linda having kept the phone in Dink's name even while he was away—and while, forty blocks away, I stood in front of the apartment building, adjusting my tie and wondering what was keeping Jock from making our rendez-vous time, over Jock's cooling body my fate was being con-structed of pieces of paper.

The Police Department didn't forgive me, but Kate did. I don't know about Bill, my thirteen-year-old son. I know he understands what happened, I do know that much, but what he thinks about it all I cannot guess. What happens in the in-terior of a child's mind is forever locked away from the com-prehension of adults. As to my forgiving myself for my multiple betrayals, I don't believe I ever will. I have adjusted to the thought of living with myself, a state of truce exists, but its permanence is still open to doubt.

Aside from its other consequences, my unmasking immo-bilized me. I could not think, could not work, could not plan for the future. In the six months since the crash we had lived on a combination of savings and Kate's part-time work at the five-and-dime.

Only now, half a year later, had I begun to do anything, and what I had begun was my construction of a wall.

And—perhaps—something else. With hope that he was bringing me something I could do—and with fear that he was bringing me something I couldn't refuse—I sat in my living room and listened to what little Wickler had to say to me. And then I agreed to go with him and have a conversation with his master, Ernie Rembek. I left a note for Bill, who would be coming home from school soon, and Wickler and I went away.

3

The doorman who came out to open the cab door knew Wickler, saluting him and saying his name and calling him Mister and Sir. Wickler preened in it, unable to resist glancing over his shoulder at me to see how I was taking it. I was irritated, and regretted having come along, which may or may not have shown in my face.

This was a new high-rise apartment building in the East Fifties, with a red canopy under which Wickler led me, and the doorman followed us into a small glass and chrome foyer with a complex control panel in the left wall as though we had entered a space ship. The doorman went to this panel, and while Wickler and I waited, used a telephone to check Wickler's admissibility and then a cream-colored plastic button to release the lock on the glass doors. We went on through.

The elevator in which we rose to the seventeenth floor continued this age-of-tomorrow feeling, its chrome walls giving back blurred Technicolor reflections of Wickler and me standing side by side and not speaking. But no matter; years ago I gave up being bitter about the comparative incomes of successful crooks and successful cops; it's a cheap and irrelevant comparison anyway, since wealth is the goal of the crook but presumably something else is the goal of the cop.

It was even more irrelevant now.

The hall was gray, the door of 17C was black. Wickler rang the bell and we waited. I felt a small itch in my spine after a moment, the sign that someone was looking at us through the peephole disguised on this door as a miniature carriage lamp, and then the door opened and we were let in by a very tall and broad young man who looked like one of those personable professional football players who makes television commercials for insurance companies.

Entering, Wickler said, "Ernie's expecting us. Tell him I brought Tobin. Uh, *Mister* Tobin."

The young man closed the door, turned flat gray eyes on me, and said, "I'll have to frisk you, sir." Very polite.

Not polite, I said, "No."

He was neither surprised nor offended. His flat gaze flicked to Wickler, who said, "It's okay. I'll take the responsibility."

He put it from his mind as though it had never been, moving to a large doorway on our left and saying, "If you'd wait in here—"

"Two minutes," I said.

Wickler said to me, "Sure thing, Mister Tobin. I'll go along and talk to Ernie myself."

I went through the large doorway into a small sitting room with furniture of a very slender and almost spindly sort, all in dark wood, an approximation of something two or three hundred years old, I suppose. I'm not much good at periods in furniture.

Left alone in there, I sat in a thin chair with spidery wooden arms and a round upholstered seat and found it surprisingly comfortable. I lit a cigarette and put the match in a round glass ashtray and looked at my watch to time the two minutes. I'd given up smoking for nearly two years, but six months ago I started again. Now this was my first cigarette since I'd decided on the wall.

In one minute and forty seconds Ernie Rembek came into the room, a narrow and amiable czar in a two-hundred-dollar suit. With vest. I'd seen him on television a few times, taking the Fifth Amendment in front of Congressional committees, but this was the first time I'd seen him in the flesh and I was surprised at how young he looked. He must be nearly fifty, but he looked hardly my age, trim and hard and lean, with sharp features and a spring to his walk. He reminded me most of those actors who portray sharp young executives in business or ad agency movies.

The smile he came in with was a complex thing, compounded of hospitality, apology, and self-satisfaction. He said, "Mister Tobin, thank you for coming. I don't imagine you want to shake hands."

That threw me off; I'd been steeling myself to the rudeness of refusing his hand. I said, "It wouldn't make sense, would it?"

"I suppose not." He shrugged easily and said, "Believe me, Mister Tobin, I appreciate your position here. I'm the enemy. It's like a retired general going to work for the Russians."

"Something like that."

"I'll try to make the arrangement no more painful than is absolutely necessary," he said. "I realize you don't want to be here, you're simply in a bind. Before we got down to business, I wanted to assure you that I do understand and I hope you'll find it possible to . . . call some kind of truce with us while this is going on."

"Wickler told me about a murder," I said.

He held up a hand to stop me, smiling apologetically. "I'm sorry, but not yet. That's business, and I never discuss business without my advisors. All I wanted to do now was thank you for coming and let you know I understood the situation and won't put any . . . unnecessary strain on you."

I know that the popular image of a syndicate chieftain is a surly overweight undereducated immigrant, and I also know that the popular image of almost everything is wrong, but still I hadn't been prepared for the charming and well-educated affability Ernie Rembek was presenting. I was off balance, and I disliked him for that almost as much as for his record. I said, "Let me worry about the strain for myself."

"Before we go into the office," he said, "I'd like to tell you a brief story. With a moral. May I?"

I shrugged. "Go ahead."

"Once when I was a kid," he said, "I took off from school one day and rode the ferry over to Staten Island. Half a dozen of us went. And coming back, you know how kids are, impatient, last one ashore's a rotten egg, all that jazz, we were crowding up front, telling the guy on duty there to go to hell, and just as we were coming in, one of the kids went over. Howie Zlotkin, his name was. He went in between the pilings and the side of the ferry. So they're backing in and out, they're trying to save the kid, and it wound up they mashed him three times between the ferry and the pilings. We're all on the rail, watching, and Howie's in the water like a pound of hamburger. Can you see the picture?"

I could, though I saw no point in it. I said, "What's the connection?"

"You," he said. "Every time I see a guy with your kind of pride, I think about Howie Zlotkin down there between the metal ferryboat and the wood pilings."

"You mean I'll be ground up."

"I've never seen it to fail," he said. "Not once. Wood and metal are tougher than skin. Anybody's skin."

I said, "You didn't tell me about Howie. What was he going home to?"

His smile was very thin. He said, "You know yourself better than most people, Mister Tobin. Come along to the office."

25

4

The office was just that, an office, with desks and phones and filing cabinets and venetian blinds, a fairly large square room set off by itself in one corner of the apartment. It already contained three men when we entered, who stood for Rembek to make the introductions.

"Mister Mitchell Tobin, this is Eustace Canfield, this is Roger Kerrigan, this is William Pietrojetti."

The three all bowed their heads in turn, and smiled me welcome, but none offered to shake my hand, and I recognized there the work of Ernie Rembek, a fast briefing before he'd come out to see me. I should have been pleased at an unpleasantness avoided, but I was not; I'd been cheated of my chance to express moral superiority by refusing to touch their hands. It did no good to remind myself that moral superiority, once expressed, has been lost. I felt cheated anyway.

Having introduced the three, Rembek now described them for me: "Canfield is my attorney, Kerrigan is an observer from the corporation, and Pietrojetti is my accountant." He waved a hand. "Sit down, gentlemen, please." More formally, he motioned me to a chair directly in front of the main desk, saying, "Would you sit here, Mister Tobin?"

I didn't like it, it put both Canfield and Kerrigan behind me, out of my range of vision. Of course, Rembek immediately sensed my dislike and its reason, and said, "But sit wherever you want," gesturing this time vaguely in the direction of a brown leather sofa along the right wall, farther away and with a clear view of the entire room.

It was time to stop permitting Rembek to treat me like an expensive race horse. I said, "No, this is fine," and sat in the chair he'd pointed to first.

I'd already seen enough anyway of the other three, sufficient to recognize their types now and their faces in the future. The attorney, Eustace Canfield, was a distinguished façade, even to the gray hair at the temples. Surely he wore a corset. He was undoubtedly a first-rate textbook lawyer with a brilliant memory and no imagination, the sort of man who can prepare a case as intricate as a house made of matchsticks but who, in court, would blunder his matchstick house into ruin.

As to Roger Kerrigan, he was a younger Ernie Rembek, a bright sharp silent young hood with a business-college education. Federal agents very often have something of the same appearance, but without the ferret eyes. And the "corporation" for which he was an observer here was the mob, the syndicate. Rembek was only a regional czar, and how he handled crises in his territory was of moment to the men at the top. Roger Kerrigan, a man who surely had no record and never would have one, a man who likely had a key to the Playboy Club and a membership at a gym, a man with a bright executive future in the "corporation," was serving here as the eyes of the men at the top. I was sure he'd do a good and thorough job.

William Pietrojetti was something else again. He wore a brown suit, as rumpled and baggy and ashes-strewn as if he'd just completed a cross-country bus trip while wearing it. He had a heavy five-o'clock shadow, and probably had one immediately after he shaved. He also had dandruff, and his black hair was a bit shaggy. He was a one-track man, obviously, the sort of accountant who in his spare time made up mathematical puzzles and sent them to *Scientific American*, whose light reading was biographies of mathematicians, and whose way with the tax laws would be a sort of intellectual rape. He would be underpaid, because his kind is always underpaid, but he wouldn't care; the only money that would interest him would be the sort he could turn into numbers on sheets of paper.

Once we were all settled down, Rembek leaned forward with his elbows on the desk and said, "How much did Wickler tell you, Mister Tobin?"

"As much as you wanted him to tell me. There's been a murder, of somebody close to you, not connected with the corporation. You want the murderer found, but not to handle him yourself. If he is found, you have no objection to his being turned over to the police."

He nodded. "That's right. And that's all he told you?"

"Yes. He wouldn't tell me why the police aren't called in anyway, since you don't mind the murderer being turned over to him at the end."

"It's a complicated situation. Before I say anything, I'll need your word that you won't ever talk about any of this on the outside."

I shook my head. "I can't promise that."

He said, "I'm not talking about covering up anything illegal."

"I don't care what you're talking about, I won't make any promises in the dark."

Canfield interrupted then, saying, "Mister Tobin, I think it would be sufficient if you would merely assure us you will treat whatever you're told here today with . . . discretion. Wouldn't that be enough for you, Ernie?"

Rembek seemed troubled. "This is important to me, Eustace," he said.

"I believe we can trust Mister Tobin's sense of fair play."

Rembek looked at me. I said, "If all you want is for me to say I won't carry gossip, I agree."

Rembek nodded curtly. "Okay," he said, "that's good enough." Then, with an obvious effort, he managed an amiable smile, saying, "This thing's very close to me. You'll understand by the time you hear it all."

"I'm willing to listen," I said.

Canfield said, "There's one last detail, Mister Tobin. A legal nicety I'd like to cover. Do you have a dollar bill handy?"

"I think so. Why?"

"I wish you to give it to me, and to state to me that you are hiring me to represent your interests in this affair."

I twisted around in my chair, the better to see him, and said, "What's that for?"

"Information exchanged between attorney and client," he said, "is a privileged communication. If at any time in the future you are asked to describe this meeting, and it is your desire to refuse, this will give you the legal grounds to do so." At the expression on my face he said, "Please, Mister Tobin, this is not shyster trickery, I assure you. I am merely making it possible for you to have the full protection of the law at some future date, should the situation arise and you desire it. By paying me the dollar you do not lose the right to talk all you want to anyone in the world. This merely gives you the choice."

I said, "But Rembek's going to tell me the story."

"No, sir, Mister Tobin, I am."

Rembek said, "Everything kosher, Mister Tobin. For your sake."

I felt obscurely like a fool but I did what they wanted, getting a dollar bill from my wallet and handing it to Canfield and asking him to represent me. He agreed gravely to do so, I went back to my chair, and he told me the details:

"Mister Rembek is a married man, Mister Tobin. I may say, a happily married man. But perhaps not entirely a faithful man. Mrs. Rembek is a somewhat nervous woman, she has her troubles, for which we are all deeply sorry, and Mister Rembek finds it necessary for his own physical and mental well-being to maintain a second establishment, where he can relax from the cares of his workaday position and enjoy the companionship of a close friend."

Rembek interrupted to say, earnestly, "I still love my wife, I want to make that clear. This has nothing to do with my wife, she's a wonderful woman."

I felt a buzzing in my nerves. If my own case were not so totally known to Rembek—to everyone in this room—surely Rembek would have said to me something along the order of man-to-man-you-understand-how-it-is. The absence of that appeal glared in the silence like an empty wall from which a painting has been stolen.

Canfield at last broke into the silence, saying, "For the last two years the close friend has been a young woman named Rita Castle, a sometime television actress. Mrs. Rembek, of course, has known nothing of the existence of Rita Castle, nor of any of her predecessors, and still knows nothing today."

"I want to keep it that way," Rembek said. "That's why I wanted you to promise to keep your mouth shut." Again he didn't say that I would understand.

Canfield said, "Mister Rembek perhaps placed too great a confidence in Miss Castle's good will. For whatever reason, he made it possible for her to put her hands on a rather large sum of money. Cash."

I said, "So she took it and ran out."

Canfield took a legal-size envelope from his pocket and

brought it over to me, saying, "Three days ago she left this note in the apartment."

It was handwritten, in green ink on gray stationery, and in rotten handwriting. I made it out with some difficulty:

I am going away. I have found a real man and we are going to find a new life together far away. You'll never see either of us again.

I said, "It's definitely from her?"

Rembek said, "Did you ever see handwriting like that before? It's her, all right. And that crack about a real man, that's her style, too."

He sounded really bitter. Looking at him, I thought it likely he'd had more genuine feeling about this close friend of his than he did for his wife, his protestations notwith-standing. It was guilt that kept him tied to his wife, but it was desire that had linked him with Rita Castle.

Canfield said, "Early this morning Miss Castle's body was found in a motel room outside Allentown, Pennsylvania. For-tunately, the motel manager has some connections with us, and when he found a reference to Mister Rembek among the effects in the young lady's purse, he called the corporation rather than the police."

I said, "Were the police ever called?"

"Not yet. If you take the job, that will be up to you, either to call them or not."

"Where's the body now?"

"Still in that motel room. Nothing has been touched."

Rembek said, bluntly, "The money's gone."

I said to him, "You think the man she went away with killed her and took the money."

"That's obvious, isn't it?"

31

"No. It's likely, but it isn't obvious. What about the motel manager, could he have taken the money? If it had been there when he went in, would he have taken it?"

Rembek looked at Kerrigan, who said, "I would say no. He's number one, trustworthy, number two, small-time, number three, nervous. Number four, he did all the right things he would have done if the money hadn't been there, and he isn't smart enough to have the money and still do all those things right."

I said, "There are other possibilities. But it's likeliest it happened the way you think. She ran off with him, he killed her, he took the money."

Rembek said, "And I want him."

I said, "For the money?"

"No."

"Because he killed her?"

Rembek shook his head. "I might have done it myself," he said, "if I'd caught up with her."

"Then why?"

"Because he *took* her. She was mine."

Canfield said smoothly, "Mister Rembek has no desire for personal vengeance, but he does wish this case cleared up as soon as possible. If he could get the money back so much the better, but the primary task is to learn the identity of the man involved. Once he is known, you may turn him over to the police with our blessing."

I said, "Then why not let the police handle it from the beginning?"

Canfield said, "Frankly, Mister Tobin, I believe the local authorities in Allentown, Pennsylvania, will have a bit of difficulty solving the case. Obviously we cannot tell them the full background, as we are telling it to you, and without the full background they are unlikely to get anywhere."

I said, "What about this apartment, where she lived? Can that be traced back to you?"

Rembek looked worriedly at Canfield, who said, "We aren't certain. We think it unlikely, but we aren't entirely sure. At the worst, Mister Rembek may be questioned, but he intends to state that he was maintaining the apartment for a friend, a man on the West Coast who does occasionally make trips East. The man in question is already prepared to support Mister Rembek's statement and claim he was loaning the apartment to Miss Castle while he was on the Coast. There is a legitimate connection between this man and Miss Castle."

Rembek said, "We hope it doesn't come up at all. If it does, we'll do our best to cover."

I said, "Finding the man may be just as difficult even with the background. Who knows how many men this girl knew? You say she was a television actress; there's all the people she might have met there, maybe other people in other ways."

Canfield said, "We think not. Take a look at that note again, Mister Tobin. You notice she says there, 'You'll never see either of us again.' *Us* again."

I saw it. I nodded and said, "You think that means the man is somebody Rembek knows."

Rembek said, "It has to be. Somebody she met through me, who got to her when my back was turned."

Kerrigan, the observer, said, "More than that. It's almost bound to be somebody inside the corporation. That's *our* main reason for wanting him found, we consider him dangerous to have around. We want him out."

Rembek explained, "The people she met through me were all people on the inside. I don't know many square johns, and the few I do know I wouldn't be bringing around that place."

I said, "Have you looked to see who's missing?"

Rembek nodded impatiently. "That's the first thing I

thought of. We got the word here at twenty after seven this morning. By twelve o'clock I'd made a list of everybody Rita knew that I knew, and by one-thirty they'd all been checked out and every one of them is where he's supposed to be."

Kerrigan said, "This guy is playing it cool. He doesn't want the corporation looking for him, so he plans to stick around for maybe a year or two, sit on the cash, and then find some nice sensible reason for retiring."

I said, "That would mean he'd planned to kill her all along He didn't plan to run away and hide with her at all."

Rembek said, "He set us both up."

Canfield, smiling faintly, said, "Do you see the multiplicity of reasons why we want him found, Mister Tobin?"

I nodded. "I see them."

"Will you take the job?"

"I don't know. What do you want me to do exactly?"

He seemed surprised. "Find him," he said.

"I mean, in detail," I said. "Do you have the idea if you hire a cop—an ex-cop—all he has to do is sit in a corner and think awhile and out comes the name?"

Canfield smiled again, saying, "Hardly, Mister Tobin. We have had some extensive dealings with the police, we do know them fairly well."

I said, "The man you want found is somewhere inside your organization. In order to find him, I'll have to get inside the organization myself. You'll have to be ready to show me anything, answer me any question."

Rembek said, "We know that. We're ready."

"I still think like a cop," I said. "I still consider myself an honest man and a responsible citizen."

Rembek said, "We *brought* you here because you're still a cop, on the inside. For every job there's a specialist, and for this job we have to go outside the company to find the specialist, and the specialist is you."

"If," Canfield said, "you'll agree to take the job."

I said, "But what I see I'll have to report. To the authorities."

Kerrigan said, "No. That isn't part of the deal. We're not here to cut our throat."

Canfield said, "Be sensible, Mister Tobin. We need a private man because we *can't* afford the scrutiny of the authorities. If you took on this job, you would have to agree that anything you might learn of the corporation's activities as a result of this employment would be treated by you in a strictly confidential and privileged manner."

"I'm not sure I can make that promise," I said.

"We cannot afford to hire you without it," he said. He leaned forward and said, "Mister Tobin, please do not let your recent unfortunate experiences make you inflexible. As an active officer on the force you found it possible to deal with informers, to make arrangements for the sake of learning the facts. This is merely the same thing. In order to do this job properly, you must be made privy to facts you would surely never learn otherwise. It would hardly be fair to take advantage of the situation by giving these facts to the authorities, now would it?"

He was right. Rigidity of mind is useless to a functioning cop. I said, "All right. If I take the job on, I'll give you the promise. If I take it on."

Canfield said, "For obvious reasons, time is a factor here. How much of it will you need before you make your decision?"

"I'll have to talk to my wife," I said. "Naturally, whatever promise of silence I make goes for my wife, too. Shell have to know what I'm doing, so I'll vouch for her now."

Canfield nodded. "That is satisfactory."

Rembek said, "Let's try to cut this as short as possible. To save you an extra trip, let's talk about the finances now, in case you decide to say yes."

"All right."

Rembek nodded to William Pietrojetti, the accountant, who until now had been so silent as to be effectively invisible. Now, in a dry and bloodless voice, Pietrojetti said to me, "The offer is five thousand dollars in advance, fifty dollars a day, reimbursement for all expenses, a maximum total of ten days on the case, and a bonus of five thousand dollars if the case is brought to a satisfactory conclusion."

Canfield said, "Of course, we'll get this all down properly on paper."

Rembek said, "Are the terms okay?"

"They're fine," I said. With five thousand dollars I could stop worrying about money for a while. Kate could quit work. And if I found the man for them it would be twice as much. Yes, the terms were okay.

Pietrojetti said, "The next question is method of payment. Do you have any preference?"

I didn't know what he meant, and told him so. He spread his hands and said, "Partly, of course, it depends on your tax structure. You should definitely report this income as income, but the project should also result in a satisfactory amount of offsetting deductions. Now, you can take the first figure as a lump-sum payment now, or we could adjust it over a two-year period if that would be better for you, or if you need the cash now but would prefer a two-year spread, we could give you the lump sum in cash and arrange paper payments to extend into January."

"I don't have that kind of tax problem," I said. "I'll take a lump sum."

He nodded, though I'm sure the answer was too simple for

him. He would have preferred to do acrobatics with the five thousand dollars for a while. Still in his dry expressionless voice, he said, "The other matter is apparent source. It is possible you would be faced with embarrassing questions if the money came overtly from us. If you'd care to, I'd be happy to go over your income potential with you in order to find the best way to insert this amount into the normal pattern."

I shook my head. "That won't be necessary. If I take this job, I won't hide it. If I'm asked, I'll tell where the money came from and what I did for it." I looked at Rembek and added, "Without giving the details."

Rembek said, "Fair enough. Is there anything else you need to know before you can make up your mind?"

"Not that I can think of."

"Fine." Rembek got to his feet, saying, "I'll have my car drive you home."

"That's all right," I said, rising, "I'll take the subway."

Rembek looked impatient. He said, "It wasn't a polite offer, Mister Tobin. If you take the job, we'll all be in a hurry. You'll want to go to Allentown, and the fastest way is in my car. The fastest way to get you home to talk to your wife is the same way."

"Oh," I said. "In that case, all right."

Rembek came around the desk, smiling slightly with one side of his mouth. "Try to relax, Mister Tobin," he said. "Nobody wants your cherry."

5

Rembek's car was a black chauffeur-driven Lincoln Continental. Sitting all alone in the back, I studied my reactions to the job I'd been offered. The job itself required no study; if it contained no elements other than those already described to me, it was a plain and honest piece of work. I might or might not be capable of handling it, but legally and morally I could have no qualms about it.

No, it wasn't the job that was complicated, it was my reaction to it. To a large extent I wanted to make believe the offer had never come along, I wanted to go back to work on my wall and think of nothing but dirt and bricks and concrete block. But in a small corner of my mind I felt a certain excitement, almost eagerness about the job; it would be a kind of return to the life I'd lost, a task within my competence, and I couldn't help feeling a degree of hunger for it.

But there was another reaction as well, a feeling of wariness and mistrust. Rembek had referred to it, crudely, at the end there, and logically I understood that he had been telling the truth, that these were businessmen and not hirelings of Satan, that they had not the slightest interest in whether or not I was in the state of grace. And yet, and yet . . . I felt very much like a yokel surrounded by slyly smiling sharpies, and I found myself time and again thinking, *What do they want from me?*

This was my first trip in a limousine, and one of the few

times I'd traveled from Manhattan home to Queens by auto, and the double novelty of this experience kept distracting me from the spiral of my thoughts. Still, by the time we'd made the turn off Woodhaven Boulevard and were sliding silently down the last four blocks to my home, I'd managed to isolate the irrational mistrust and put it away in a box where it wouldn't confuse my mind. I would make my decision without that.

I pointed out the house, and the chauffeur pulled to a stop directly behind my Chevrolet. I felt awkward climbing out of such a car in front of my own house; the car couldn't have looked more out of place parked in front of an igloo. I went on up the walk to the house.

I'd called Kate at the store before leaving Rembek's apartment, telling her only that I had something to discuss with her and wanted her to come home right away, and she met me now at the front door, looking past me and saying, "Did you come here in *that?*"

"It's part of the story," I said.

"Come to the kitchen," she said. "I put coffee on."

We walked along the hall past the stairs. I said, "Where's Bill?"

"I don't know, out somewhere. Will you be having dinner?"

"I don't know yet. It depends."

I sat at the kitchen table and told her the story while she made me coffee and got out a plate of chocolate chip cookies. She sat opposite me as I finished the story, and then said, "Do you want to do it, Mitch?"

"I don't know. I've been thinking I have to get work, sooner or later I need a job of some kind. This could tide us over for a while. And it's one employer who won't ask a lot of questions."

"Mitch, please. Don't make money decide for you, I've told you I don't mind doing my share, and I mean it."

"This isn't your share."

"Don't decide because of money," she said. "Please, Mitch, promise me you won't."

"In other words, you don't want me to do it."

She shook her head. "No. As a matter of fact, I do want you to do it. But not for the money, that would be the wrong reason."

"What's the right reason?"

"You were stopped," she said. "Six months ago you just came to a stop, as though somebody turned a switch. Maybe this will get you started again."

I got up from the table and went over to the back door and out onto the porch. Under the long shadows of late afternoon, the hole looked like a grave again. I had the piles of brick covered with canvas tarps, gray anonymous mounds out there like cancerous mushrooms. But that was where I wanted to be, bending my back, working my arms and my shoulders, thinking about shovelfuls of dirt, thinking about the arc of the pick, checking the depth of the hole, watching the level, filling my mind with the details of the wall, filling it so full with the facts of the wall that no space could be left over for anything else.

For the money, then. And because it would make Kate hopeful.

I went back into the kitchen. "I'll have to pack some clothes," I said. "I don't know how long I'll have to stay in Allentown."

6

Allentown is about ninety miles due west of New York. We drove back into Manhattan, picked up Roger Kerrigan, the observer, at Third Avenue and 34th Street, and an hour and twenty minutes later we swung off Route 22 outside Allentown and came to a stop on the gravel in front of the Mid-Road Motel.

Kerrigan, at first, had tried to make smalltalk, mentioning baseball and movies and so on, trying to find some subject in which I would be interested, but I had no desire to talk with him and couldn't make the effort to be polite, so after a while he'd grown silent and we hurtled westward in our separate rear corners of the limousine.

The Mid-Road Motel was cheap but new, its tinsel still bright and seeming nearly to be a sufficient substitute for quality. We had passed similar places, a bit older, which had made it clear how badly this structure would age, but for the moment it was sparkling and cheerful and the limousine did not look entirely incongruous in front of it.

The owner, whom we found in his office, was a short round nervous man with a bushy mustache and a receding hairline, a man of about forty, who, I would judge, had failed in small business enterprises in the past and would do so again in the future. His name was William MacNeill, and he was expecting us. When Kerrigan introduced himself, MacNeill bustled right into action, grabbing a key from the board and coming around the end of the desk, saying, "I'll

41

show you where she is." We followed him back outside.

It was just six o'clock. To the left an access road led up to Route 22, which ran, four lanes wide, straight as a ruler into the sun sitting on the horizon out at about Harrisburg. The big trucks rolled by up there at sixty miles an hour, their aluminum sides casting sheets of orange sun reflection. All shadows were very long and very thin and very pale.

We walked along the stucco front of the motel, past the pastel doors, each with its silver number. The sun was in our eyes, making us lower our heads like a trio of penitents. Venetian blinds were drawn in the window beside each door.

"I haven't touched her," MacNeill told us over his shoulder. "Haven't moved her. Haven't touched a thing."

The door he unlocked was numbered 9 and had a *Do Not Disturb* sign hanging on the knob. MacNeill took the sign off, saying, "I put that there myself. Make sure nobody else went in."

He hit a light switch as he went in, then stepped to one side for Kerrigan and me, shutting the door behind us.

It was a long narrow room with plain beige walls, no molding, rust carpet on the floor. At this end there were the door and window, and a radiator enclosure under the window. At the far end, a closet on the left, bathroom on the right. In between were two beds, their heads against the right-hand wall, separated by a simulated wood night table with a modernistic lamp on it. There was little space to get by between the foot of each bed and the left wall. Nearer us, also on the right wall, was a long low dresser, also of simulated wood, with a large wall mirror above it, and a small upholstered chair with flat wooden arms. Beyond the beds, toward the bathroom, were a small dark writing table and wooden chair. The left wall was bare, except for a long painting of woods in autumn placed at about the midpoint. The painting looked like jigsaw puzzles I'd done as a boy.

At first the room gave an appearance of complete normality. A small white suitcase lay open on the dresser, showing an interior filled with female garments. A pair of black high heels stood neatly beside the near bed. A white bath towel was flung across the far bed. Only one bed had been slept in and it was still rumpled.

But there was blood on the towel, just a little, just barely noticeable, a streak of stain across it like rust. And the drawer was missing from the night table between the beds.

MacNeill walked down the room and stopped, looking in at the floor between the beds. "Here she is here," he said.

Kerrigan apparently had no desire to observe this part. He stood to one side, and I went forward and stood beside MacNeill and gazed down at her.

They always look dead. That may be a stupid thing to say, but it's true. I've seen the imitations, in the movies and on television, and I've seen the real thing in the course of my former job, and there's never any question about it. The real corpse looks like something that never was alive.

It lay face down, naked, its arms stretched out ahead of it like an acrobat still reaching for the trapeze. The back of its head was punched in, the blond hair now matted with rust. The rest of the body, as much of it as I could see, was untouched. It looked as though she had come out fresh from the shower, had started to go around between the beds, and had been struck down by one hard vicious blow from behind.

In falling, her flailing hand had hooked in the handle of the night-table drawer, yanking it out and onto the floor, where it lay beside the body like a box for offerings. It had contained stationery and a Gideon Bible; the stationery was now scattered around the body, and the Bible was tilted face down against the corpse's left elbow.

MacNeill said, "You want me to turn her over?"

"No. Don't touch anything." I looked around. "All her effects are here?"

"Yes, sir," he said eagerly. "She just had that one little suitcase there, and a purse."

"Where's the purse?"

"I put it in the safe, in the office."

"Where was it? When you came in here, where did you find it?"

"On the dresser, right beside the suitcase."

"Before we call the police, put it back where it was."

MacNeill licked his lips and glanced toward Kerrigan. "We're going to call the cops?"

Kerrigan shrugged. "If he says so. He's the boss."

"I was hoping—"

Kerrigan said, "You think the publicity's going to hurt? It's going to *help*, pal. Everybody'll want to stay at the murder motel."

Hopefully, MacNeill said, "You think so?"

I walked on back to the bathroom and glanced inside it. There was a soap wrapper in the wastebasket, nothing more. In the closet were a lot of wire hangers, two holding dresses and one holding a pair of slacks. Nothing on the shelf. A pair of woman's loafers on the floor. Nothing in the loafers. A pair of stockings hung over a hook on the closet's rear wall.

I took a quick look around the room, while MacNeill and Kerrigan watched me, and found nothing of interest. When I was done I said, "All right. This is all of it?"

"There's her car, too."

"Her car?"

"It's still out front," MacNeill said. "A little pale blue Mustang."

"Let's go look at it."

Outside, white lines on the blacktop showed where the guests should angle-park their cars facing the doors of the rooms. The pale blue Mustang was neatly between its white lines, clean and alert, windows rolled down, ready to spurt away as needed. The sun had set completely now, and there was a kind of grayish-green light in the air. Up atop the slope the big rigs still rumbled east and west. A car was just pulling in beside the limousine down at the other end of the motel, near the office. Seeing me look at it, MacNeill said, "My wife'll take care of them."

"I'll want to talk to her later," I said.

"Yes, sir."

The interior of the Mustang had nothing to offer beyond a pair of white gloves in the glove compartment and a copy of the *Atlantic Monthly* on the back seat. But when I went around to the back the keys were there, stuck into the trunk lock.

MacNeill said, "Look at that! I didn't notice that before."

"Did you come around this end of the car before?"

"No."

"Then they were here." I said to Kerrigan, "She had the money in the trunk, in another suitcase or a bag or something. He was in too much of a hurry to go put the keys back in her purse."

MacNeill said, "But he went and took the room key with him."

"Not very far," I said. "He would have thrown it into some grass somewhere along the line." A stout woman, jangling keys, was coming toward us, followed at a snail's pace by the new car, an elderly black Buick with a very nervous young couple in it. I said to MacNeill, "Where can we sit and talk?"

"We have an apartment in back of the office," he said. To the stout woman, just then reaching us, he said, "Betsy, these

45

are the men from New York. They want to talk to you when you get a minute."

Betsy—which was a bad name for her—had the beetle-browed look of a woman who's spent years driving her man the way skinners drive mules and who has been worn out by it. She gave us a graceless nod of acknowledgment, said, "When I get a chance," and plodded on by us. We stepped out of the way of the Buick, which passed us with the young couple blinking constantly and looking straight ahead.

We walked on back to the office, where MacNeill led us around behind the counter and through a curtained doorway into a small living room crammed with bulky furniture which twenty years ago had been purchased for a room twice this size. MacNeill sat us down and then tried to play host for a minute or two, offering us coffee, beer, ashtrays, a drink, whatever we wanted, until I said, "What I want is to talk to you for a minute."

"I'm sorry," he said. "Of course, you're right." He sat down at once and clasped his hands in his lap.

I said, "What kind of description can you give me of the man?"

He blinked. "What man?"

"The man she came with," I said.

"Oh, no," he said. "She came by herself. She said somebody would be meeting her in a couple of days, but if he ever showed up I didn't see him."

Kerrigan said, "From the looks of things, he showed up."

MacNeill said, "Is that right? You think he was the one?"

I said, "When did she get here?"

"Monday. Just about this time."

It was now Thursday. I said to Kerrigan, "Would that be right? When did she take off?"

"Our friend found the note Monday night. He'd seen her Saturday night."

"All right." I looked back at MacNeill. "So she came here Monday. Did she pick this place because she knew you were connected with the mob or was it just coincidence?"

MacNeill winced at the word "mob," so I suppose whatever he did in that area of his life he'd worked out a good rationalization for it, one in which he wasn't *really* connected with the mob.

It was Kerrigan who answered me, saying, "Rembek does a lot of traveling. He might have stopped here with her once or twice and she remembered it. She wouldn't have known about any link-up."

MacNeill nodded eagerly, glad of something to talk about. "That's right," he said, "Mister Rembek has stopped here several times. I don't know if this particular young lady was ever with him, but I do remember Mister Rembek. He has a car like the one you gentlemen came in."

I said, "Back to the girl. What name did she use?"

"Rita Manners."

I asked him to spell the last name, which he did, and then Kerrigan asked me what difference the spelling made. I said, "None in particular. She was just doing a pun, and I wondered how far she pushed it."

"A pun?"

"Her name was Castle. A castle's a big house. So's a manor. Rita Manor. But she didn't want a name that called attention to itself, so she made it Rita Manners, with the normal spelling."

"What difference does it make?"

"It tells me something about who she was," I said. "It may help to know about her, so I can maybe figure out what would have been her idea of a real man."

47

He made a blunt suggestion. I said, "No. Already I know she was more complicated than that."

MacNeill's wife came in, then, making the room seem even smaller than before, and muttering to no one in particular, "If those two are married I'm the Queen of Sheba."

MacNeill patted the sofa beside himself, saying, "Sit down, Betsy."

She settled with an audible grunt, thudding backward into the seat and then adjusting herself, pulling the faded skirt down over her thick knees. "If the bell rings," she said, "I'll have to go get it."

"This won't take long," I said. "Which one of you checked the girl in?"

MacNeill said, "I did."

"How long did she take the room for?"

"Just one day at a time. Each morning she came and paid for another day."

"Did she ever talk with either of you?"

"Chatted like a magpie with me when I was changing the linen," the wife said. "Asking me about movie houses, how did I like Allentown, had I ever been out West, all of that."

Mrs. MacNeill had clearly disliked Rita Castle, but I thought I could put that down to impersonal jealousy, the junkman's nag hating the passing thoroughbred. I said, "Did she spend a lot of time in her room?"

She said, "Nearly all. I think she went out to a movie or somewheres Tuesday night, she asked me what was playing down in town, but that was all."

MacNeill said, "There's a diner just down the street here to the right, the opposite way from the highway. We usually send our guests there if they ask for a place, and that's where she had all her meals."

"That we know of," said Mrs. MacNeill.

48

I said to her, "Do you think she went other places?"

But it had just been the innuendo of jealousy. She said, "No, I guess not. Spent all her time right here. Waiting for somebody."

"A man," I said. "And neither of you saw him show up?"

Mrs. MacNeill said, "This time of year, we can count on filling up by eleven, eleven-thirty. We're in bed ourselves by midnight, our room's back through there. If anybody came in after that, we wouldn't hear it unless they rang the bell by the office door."

"All right," I said. "Now I'd like to see her purse."

MacNeill got it and handed it to me. It was a white doeskin pouch, a larger version of a medieval purse, with a thong drawstring to close the top. Inside were the usual paraphernalia, tissues and lipstick and compact and books of matches and so on, plus a wallet of the same pale blue as the Mustang.

The wallet added a number of facts. It contained a driver's license which gave me her age—twenty-four—and her physical description. Also current membership cards in two of the actors' unions, Screen Actors Guild and American Federation of Television and Radio Artists, SAG and AFTRA. Also an outdated membership card in the third actors' union, Equity, the union for performers in legitimate theater. Also a New York Public Library card from the Cathedral Branch on Lexington Avenue. Also three pictures of children, smiling and squinting in bright sunlight somewhere where the land is very flat and treeless and the horizon is far away.

When I was done with the purse, I gave it back to MacNeill and told him, "Be sure and put it back before you call the police."

Mrs. MacNeill began to complain at once, objecting to the idea of police. Why didn't we merely take the body away and hide it somewhere?

I said, "I was hired to find out who did this. It will help me if the police are brought in. Their lab men and technicians may pick up a lot of information in that room that I couldn't possibly get myself." I glanced at Kerrigan and said, "And I imagine you people have channels to get their information back to me."

He nodded. "Whatever they know," he said, "you'll know five minutes later."

Mrs. MacNeill said, a whine in her voice, "You put us in an awful bad position, mister. How do we explain how come we didn't call them right away?"

"You do call them right away," I said. "I don't like having to fake any of the circumstances, but it will throw them off less if we do. If we tried telling the truth, the investigating officers would get off on a bad tangent right away and they might never get back on the track."

"So what do we do?"

"You make one small change. Yesterday Miss Castle paid for *two* days. She came in and said, 'Looks like I'll be here longer than I thought,' and she paid two days in advance. You change that on your books."

MacNeill nodded. "That's no problem," he said.

"This morning," I said, "the Do Not Disturb sign was hanging on the door, so you didn't go in to change the linen. In fact, you still haven't." I looked at my watch: six-twenty. "About nine o'clock tonight," I said, "you will be sufficiently worried and disturbed to take a chance on opening the door. You'll find the body, and you'll immediately call the police. And *do* it, go through the whole thing. Go down to that room and knock on the door and call her name and very reluctantly open the door. Come out nervous and upset and run back to the office to make the call."

MacNeill said, "In case somebody's watching."

50

"Right. And the only thing unusual that happened today was that a chauffeur-driven limousine stopped, the two passengers started to take a room, looked at it first, and changed their mind. Mention that only if you're asked."

"Yes, sir." MacNeill was smiling with relief, seeing how it could all get straightened out after all.

Kerrigan said, "What about us? Do we stay here or what?"

I said, "No. We may want to come back in a day or two, I don't know. Right now we want to get back to the city."

Before we left, I said to MacNeill, "Remember not before nine o'clock. I need time to get some things done at the other end."

He promised, and we went out to the car and headed back for New York.

7

The apartment in which Rita Castle had been maintained was
two blocks south and one half block east of Ernie Rembek's official residence. I wondered if he had ever walked it.

The building was similar to the other, and the apartment
was on an even higher floor, the twenty-third. A very wide
living room had broad drape-framed windows facing west,
giving a panoramic view of midtown high over the black
bunched tops of the brownstones that filled out the block
westward, looking from way up here like pieces in a grimy
Monopoly game. Wine and white were the dominant colors
in the room, with wine carpeting and a white sofa the largest
blocks of color. A large op art abstraction in shades of gray,
with white lines, stood all alone on one long off-white wall.
The wall opposite was broken up with doors and doorways,
leading to—in order from the entrance—a closet, a small but
beautifully equipped kitchen, and a long narrow bedroom
with its own panoramic view of the city. A tiny green bathroom with a shower but no tub was off the bedroom. From its
position, and the presence of a fan high in one wall, I assumed
it shared an airshaft with the kitchen, since neither had any
windows.

The living room was as impersonal as a psychiatrist's
office and as luxurious as a resort hotel, but in the bedroom
Rita Castle had permitted herself some expression of individ-
uality. The Hollywood bed was covered by a patchwork quilt

that looked oddly innocent and old-fashioned and which had certainly been homemade. The shelf at the bottom of the night table was stacked full of a sloppy pile of books and magazines. There were copies of *Atlantic*, *The New Yorker*, *Harper's*, *Evergreen Review*, *Playboy* and *Cosmopolitan*. The books, all paperback, included no fiction of any kind, but were fact books of a wide assortment, ranging from studies of Greek mythology through surveys of nymphomania and Lesbianism to biographies of current political figures.

On the bed itself were two more pieces of reading matter: last week's *Variety* and the magazine section of last Sunday's *Times*, the latter open to the crossword puzzle, which had been about half filled in. And, finally, on the floor at the foot of the bed was a stack of hardcover editions of Broadway plays.

The bedroom also contained a vanity table and a dresser, both full of things appropriate to a young woman whose looks were of paramount importance. Tucked in a corner of the bottom drawer of the dresser were some letters from Rita Castle's mother, postmarked East Grange, South Dakota. The letters were newsy, but here and there they betrayed the mother's uneasiness that her daughter's life in New York City contained elements that were being hidden from the family. There were no references to anyone at all in New York; if Rita had mentioned any of her city friends in her own letters, the mother showed no sign of it.

There was a pastel-blue telephone on the night table, with an address book beside it, containing surprisingly few entries. I copied down what names, addresses, and phone numbers there were, and put the address book back where I'd found it.

The kitchen contained one more book; the *I Hate To Cook Book*, by Peg Bracken. Refrigerator and cabinet contained only foods that could be prepared quickly and with a minimum of bother; it was obvious that no real meals were ever eaten here.

Piled on the shelf in the bedroom closet were television and movie scripts, each with certain lines underlined in red pencil; apparently Rita Castle actually had done some acting from time to time, though financially she obviously didn't have to.

Kerrigan sat patiently in the living room until I was finished. We'd entered the apartment at five to eight, and by twenty to nine I was done. "All right," I said. "That's all here."

Kerrigan got to his feet and stretched, saying, "You getting anywhere?"

"I'm starting," I said. "Did you know this girl?"

He shrugged. "I saw her with Ernie a few times."

"What did you think of her?"

"I don't know. She acted like the original dumb bunny, you know? The real feeble-minded broad. But I think it was a put-on."

"For Rembek?"

"Maybe partly. I think she was a sharp girl; I think down inside there she had a quick brain. Sometimes I thought she was doing the dumb bunny as a put-on for herself."

"Playing the part."

"Right."

"Do you have the note she left?"

"No, Ernie has that."

"I want to see it again. As I remember it, it had that dumb-bunny sound. It didn't lead me to expect . . ." I gestured toward the bedroom. "She was more complicated than the note sounded."

"I never thought she rang a hundred-percent true," Kerrigan said. "But she wasn't any trouble, and if she got a kick out of putting Ernie on, that was up to them."

"Get me the note, all right?"

"Will do. Where do we go from here?"

"I go home. You go back to Rembek and get some more things set up. First you arrange it so the police do get to Rembek through this apartment, and they get to him right away. Then he can give them the story about his friend on the West Coast."

"You've got a reason for this?"

"Yes. I want to cover myself, not to get myself off any hooks but just to keep myself from being a red herring for the investigating officers. I want them to be able to concentrate on the killing itself and not waste their time wondering what I'm up to."

"Fine. How do we do that?"

I said, "This morning the man on the West Coast phoned Rembek, he said the girl who'd been staying in his apartment seemed to have disappeared. There wasn't anything between him and the girl, but he did wonder if there was any trouble she was in or anything like that and would Rembek, being right here in town, check it out for him. Rembek said yes, had people look around, and when it seemed as though the girl really had disappeared, he hired me to look for her. That's why I went to see Rembek this afternoon and why Rembek's chauffeur drove me home. This evening I talked long-distance with the man on the West Coast—you'll have to get me his name—from Rembek's apartment, and then I came here and looked around. I will now go home and call a friend of mine in Missing Persons and see if anybody has reported her missing."

"The answer will be no."

"I know that. As soon as the police get to Rembek, I want him to call me and tell me the girl's been found dead. I want him then to hire me to help look for the killer."

Kerrigan smiled. "Everything neat and tidy, huh?"

"I don't want to muddy the waters if I can avoid it," I said.

"Sure. Okay, I'll go over and set that up right now. You want the car to drive you home?"

"Yes. I brought that suitcase along, I'd rather not tote it on the subway. It'll be less obvious than having me walk down my block carrying it. I don't have an explanation for it, so I'd rather no neighbor noticed it, just in case some completist decides to ask questions around my area."

We went down in the elevator together, Kerrigan spoke to the chauffeur, and then we separated, he walking up toward the corner, I getting into the car.

After we went through the Midtown Tunnel and got on the Long Island Expressway, I leaned forward and said to the chauffeur, "Have you been driving for Mister Rembek long?"

"Yes, sir. About three years."

He was about thirty, black-haired, with a strong-looking and somewhat heavy body. His face was dominated by a large Mussolini-type jaw, which gave him a stupid look, but when he spoke his manner was brisk and educated.

I said, "Did you know the woman who lived in the building we were just in?"

"Miss Castle? Yes, sir."

"Did you sometimes drive her places without Mister Rembek?"

"Yes, sir, very often. Shopping, or to rehearsals when she was in television shows, or going downtown to see her old friends."

"What did you think of her?"

He glanced at me warily in the rear-view mirror. "I'm not sure I can answer that, sir," he said.

"You can. It won't get back to Mister Rembek. I need to

know as much as I can about her."

"Yes, sir." He hesitated, then said, "Well, I would say . . . I would say she was a dangerous girl, sir."

"Dangerous?"

"She was, uh, I suppose, bored, sir. She didn't know what to do with herself a lot of the time."

"You mean she made passes at you."

He looked embarrassed. "It sounds sort of dumb when you say it that way."

"But she did."

"Yes, sir. Sort of."

"Sort of?"

"Well, it was more like a game she was playing. I think she only did it because she could be sure I wouldn't take her up on it. I figure she didn't want me to take her up on it."

"Did you?"

"Who, me?" He seemed really surprised. "I know when I'm well off!"

"What do you think she would have done, if you had responded?"

"Hollered her head off. Got me some lumps."

"Rembek wouldn't have been happy."

"Mister Rembek would have wanted my balls, sir."

"Okay. Thank you."

"Yes, sir." After a minute he said, "Sir, this what I said, this won't get back to Mister Rembek, will it?"

"No. It's none of his business."

"Thank you, sir."

We rode the rest of the way in silence. When we got to the house I hurried inside with the suitcase and found Kate and Bill in the living room, watching a spy show on television. I told Kate I wouldn't be staying away after all, at least not now, and then I went upstairs to make my phone call to Eddie

57

Schultz, a guy I went through Police Academy with who now works in the Missing Persons Bureau. I called him at home and ignored the strain in his voice as we went through the necessary it's-been-too-long-we've-got-to-get-together-sometime preliminaries. Then I asked him my question: "Could you find out for me if there's been any report of a young woman named Rita Castle on the missing list? Actress, lives in Manhattan."

"I could find out for you. Where are you, at home?"

"Yes."

"I'll call you back."

"Thanks, Eddie."

I went back down to the living room and found that Kate had gone out to the kitchen to make me a cup of coffee. I sat down and tried to chat with Bill about school, but it was hard work. He was willing to talk, open and amiable with me, but I felt the strain in my own voice, and my thoughts were distracted by the constant questions in my head: What is he thinking? What does he think of me? What is in his mind about me? But if there was anything to learn, I knew of no way to learn it.

Eddie called back a few minutes later, and I was thankful for the interruption. He told me there was no such name as Rita Castle on the list, and I thanked him and went back to the living room. Kate was there now, and so was my coffee.

I drank the coffee, looking at the television screen without really seeing it, and then I went out to the emotional calm of the backyard. With the porch light on, there was enough illumination for me to do a little more digging, though I couldn't do the finishing work, the leveling and smoothing and measuring. But I did get some work done, and cleared my mind, and felt somewhat better.

I came in at eleven o'clock, shortly after Bill had called

goodnight to me out the back door. Kate and I sat at the kitchen table and I told her what I'd done, what I'd thought, what I'd learned. She handed me an envelope and told me a man had brought it to the house a little after six. Inside it was a check for five thousand dollars, made out to me and drawn on the account of something called Continental Projects, Incorporated, with a Grand Central Terminal box number for an address. On the left side of the check face there was a space for the check's purpose to be written in, and in that space had been typed the words "For Professional Services."

I wrote my name on the back and gave it to Kate to put in the account in the morning. All I felt by now was tired, and a little later I went upstairs to bed.

8

The call came at nine-thirty in the morning. I was at work on my wall again when Kate came out on the porch and said, "There's someone on the phone for you."

It was Rembek himself. He said, "Well, they came to see me."

I said, "Who?"

"Two detectives."

"What about?"

"Huh?"

"Two detectives came to see you about what?"

"About the girl, what do you think?"

"What about the girl?" I asked him.

He finally understood. He gave a sigh of exasperation and said, "Okay, Mister Tobin, we'll do it your way." He then told me Rita Castle had been found murdered in Allentown, Pennsylvania, and he had been empowered by George Lewis, the man in Los Angeles, to make private inquiries into the details of her murder. I agreed to take the job, and he said with a touch of sarcasm in his voice that he was glad to hear it.

I said, "Now I'm going to need two things."

"Name them."

"First, an office in Manhattan. Someplace small. All I need is a room with a desk and a phone."

"No problem. What's the other thing?"

"I want you to make a list of everybody you know who also

knew Rita Castle. I want the name and address and phone number and occupation."

"That's the list of suspects, right?"

I said, "We're starting off with the assumption that the way she phrased her note meant the man was someone you knew. For the moment, we'll make the further assumption that you also knew that she and this man were acquainted. So that's the list we'll make now. If it isn't any of those people, we'll have to change our assumptions."

Rembek said, "Is this the way cops always work?"

"Part of it."

He laughed and said, "Then how come I'm a free man?"

"You have a lot of money."

"That's right," he said soberly. "That's the edge, isn't it? All right, Mister Tobin, I'll make up that list right now. You'll hear within the hour about your office. You want the car today?"

"Not now. I don't know about later on."

"Let me give you the number you can call if you want it. The chauffeur's name is Dominic Brono."

He gave me a Plaza number, which I wrote down. I said, "Can I reach you at this number, too?"

"No. I'll be at this number here most of the time. If I'm out, you can get a message to me through here."

He gave me that number, too, and then we both hung up.

I immediately called the Missing Persons Bureau and asked for Eddie Schultz, knowing he'd be on duty now. When he came on, I said, "I just got word about that girl, the one I asked you about last night. She was found killed."

"Killed? Here in Manhattan?"

"No. Someplace in Pennsylvania. But she was connected with Ernie Rembek some way, so I suppose our people will get involved in it."

61

He said, "Mitch, what's your connection with this?"

"Rembek hired me yesterday to look for her."

"You going into the private detective business, Mitch?"

I said, "No." You need a license in New York State to operate as a private detective. Even if I wanted to I couldn't see myself applying for such a license, not with my record. I said, "It was strictly off-the-cuff, to use my experience and contacts to see if I could make the girl turn up."

"You think Rembek bumped her off? And he's trying to use you as part of an alibi, maybe?"

I'd thought of that myself, and rejected it for a number of reasons. I said, "I don't know, Eddie, could be. It isn't likely, though. Anyway, Rembek wants me to keep interested in it."

"The Homicide people won't like that, Mitch."

"I'll keep my place," I said.

"Okay. Don't make trouble for yourself, fella."

He was truly concerned for me; old friendships die hard. I said, "I'll watch myself, Eddie. Thanks."

Then I went out to the yard again to work on my wall while waiting for the detectives to show up.

9

They came shortly before noon, quite a while after I got the second call from Rembek, in which he informed me my office was at 493 Fifth Avenue, room 703. I should ask the elevator operator for the key. The list I'd asked for would be in the desk drawer. If I wanted anything else I should just holler.

The Police Department is rarely subtle, but this time they did show a certain subtlety: two plainclothes men came to see me, one a stranger and the other an old friend. That way, they were ready to take any tack with me that might be necessary, depending on how I behaved.

I behaved like a man who wants to co-operate. The three of us sat in the living room, they politely declined Kate's offer of coffee, and we settled down to talk.

The one I knew was Marty Kengelberg. We'd worked out of the same precinct for seven years, before he got reassigned to Manhattan Homicide South. He introduced the other one as "my partner, Fred James." We didn't shake hands.

Marty said, "I suppose you know what we're here for."

"You want to talk about Rita Castle," I said.

"Right. Tell me the story, Mitch."

So I told him the story. It didn't entirely have the ring of realism, but that couldn't be helped. The truth was equally unreal-sounding.

When I was done, Marty cautioned me against operating as a private detective, and I told him I intended to be careful about that. Then he asked me how much Rembek was paying me, and when I said five thousand dollars, he and Fred James looked at one another and James was the one to ask the next question, saying, "That's a lot of money for such a vague job. How you supposed to earn it?"

"I don't think I will earn it," I said. "It was their figure, not mine."

James said, "Why do *they* think it's worth so much?"

"I think Rembek was hung on the girl. He says not, but I think he was. I think at first he figured she'd ducked out on him and what he wanted was to get her back. He's got more money than he knows what to do with. I can see him saying to himself, 'I'd give five grand to get Rita back.' And then looking around for somebody to give the five grand to."

"And you were there."

"Right."

James made that delicate eyebrow motion that means you're-a-liar. He said, "That was very lucky for you."

"I don't think it was luck," I said. "My name got pretty well known six months ago, so when Rembek decided what he wanted was an ex-cop, I was the one he thought of. I took the job because I need the money."

James said, "It's the job that has me a little confused. What are you supposed to do? I mean, generally speaking."

"I'm doing it now," I said. "Generally speaking."

Marty said, "Take it easy, Mitch. You know we've got to do this."

"Of course. I think what Rembek wants is a kind of liaison between him and the Police Department. I think the girl meant so much to him that now he feels he wants to be right on top of the investigation. Also, there's one other thing."

James said, "There's always one other thing."

This was the first time I'd been on this end of the hard-soft routine and I could see now why it was so effective. I made an effort to ignore James, turned back to Marty and said, "Rembek thinks there's a possibility she was killed by somebody in his mob. If so, he's in a bind. He can't invite you boys in to snoop around without making trouble for himself, but if he keeps you out, the guy who killed Rita Castle may never be found."

Marty said, "So he wants you to do the investigation in the mob."

"Right. I've agreed not to use anything else I might learn, and they've agreed if the killer does turn out to be one of theirs, I can go ahead and turn him over to you."

James said, "That's sporting of you."

Marty said, "What I can't get over is how you were hired the day *before* she was found. She was already dead by then, but she wasn't found yet."

I said, "I really don't think Rembek is trying to set up a false trail or anything like that. So far as I can judge, he's clean. I wouldn't have taken the job otherwise."

James said, "What's that hole for, out in your backyard?"

I looked at Marty. I said, "Marty, can we skip this scene? I already know all the lines."

Marty said, "Mitch, you just don't fit in the picture. Don't blame Fred, he's trying to figure out what you're doing here. So am I."

James said, "If you don't want to tell me about the hole you don't have to. It's your privilege."

I said, "Is there anything else, Marty?"

He said, "Yes. Don't try to use friendship, Mitch."

I got to my feet. "Don't come back without a warrant, you bastard."

James said, "Keep cool, friend."

Kate came into the room then, saying, "Is something wrong, Mitch?"

"No. Marty and his friend were just leaving."

Marty got slowly to his feet and a second later so did James. Marty said, "I guess you've forgotten what the job is, Mitch. I'm not doing anything here you wouldn't do, not anything you haven't done a hundred times yourself."

I said, "What you've forgotten is who I am. There are questions you can ask me and know the answer is absolutely going to be straight. You used to know that."

Marty glanced at Kate, and then hesitated, and then went ahead anyway: "You forfeited that, Mitch. When you weren't there to back up Jock."

Kate said, "Marty!"

"No," I said to her. "He had the right to say that. He didn't have the need, but he did have the right."

Marty said, "Mitch, I'll ask you a question, one that deserves a straight answer. Are you holding anything back?"

I said, "You're asking me in front of your partner? If I say yes, you can put me away as a material witness till it's all over."

"Okay. Fred, I'll be out in a minute."

James nodded. He said to me with heavy sarcasm, "Nice to've met you, Tobin." Then Kate went with him to the door.

Marty said, "Well? Are you holding anything back?"

"Yes."

"Why?"

"My judgment. I don't want to confuse the issue."

"What are you holding back, Mitch?"

"I'm not sure I can trust you any more."

"Then we're even. What are you holding back?"

I said, "The body was found fourteen hours before. That motel has a tie-in with the mob. When the owner saw Rembek's name in the girl's purse he called the mob instead of the law. She was Rembek's girl and she ducked out and she took some cash with her. I suppose unreported income. Rembek hired me to find the guy, both to get even and to get his money back. I said the murder had to be reported. I was the one who set up the second discovery. To keep it simple."

Marty nodded. "All right, that makes more sense. It didn't feel right, you being hired a day early. You went out there yesterday?"

"Yes. Nothing was touched, not by me or anybody else. The rediscovery made no substantive change. And if the couple at the motel had reported finding a body and waiting fourteen hours to report it, you'd all be wasting your energies now on a lot of irrelevancies."

"We are anyway," he said.

"You can stop now."

He said, "And you're going to run an investigation inside the mob, is that it?"

"That's what Rembek wants. If I find anything I'll turn it right over to you."

"Good. You understand, I can't make the same offer. What we learn we'll have to keep to ourselves."

"I know that."

"All right. Thanks for giving me the straight story."

"I always will, Marty."

"Sure." He turned away, then looked back and said, "Forget that crack I made, will you?"

"I'll try."

"Yeah. So long."

After he left, Kate came in and said, "You want a cup of coffee? Are you going to work out back?"

"No, I don't have time now. I'll phone you later." I put on a tie and jacket and took the subway to Manhattan.

10

My office was a small high-ceilinged room in a very old building across the street from the main library on Fifth Avenue. There was one dusty window with venetian blinds; looking down from it I could see Fifth Avenue, the shoppers walking, the buses and taxis angling back and forth like a gully of magnets, and off to the right the intersection of Fifth Avenue and 42nd Street. Across the street was the huge Greek mausoleum of a library, with its steps and stone lions.

My office was lit by one gigantic globe light hanging far down from the ceiling. Dark green metal shelves had been built on three walls and now stood dusty and empty. The desk was small, wooden, and scarred, with a matching swivel chair. There was a large four-drawer filing cabinet behind the desk, and on a small wheeled metal stand to the left of the desk was an electric typewriter with a sticker on it saying it was rented from Eagle Typewriter & Adding Machine. A wooden chair stood off to one side, and next to the typing stand was a metal wastebasket. That was it for the furniture.

Atop the desk was a black telephone, as dusty as everything else in the room. In the top side drawer of the desk was a stack of white paper, a large yellow legal-size pad, a ballpoint pen, and five new freshly sharpened pencils. The other side drawers were empty, but the center drawer contained a sheet of paper with the list I'd asked Rembek for. There were ten names, each with an address and phone number and occupation, all typed neatly in a row. I looked at them, and then called Rembek. When he came on the line, I said, "I'm in the office."

"Is it okay?"

"Yes, but the list isn't."

"The list I sent over? What's wrong with it?"

"It doesn't have Dominic Brono's name on it."

"What? My *chauffeur?*"

"He knew Rita. He drove her places, on your orders."

"You think it was *him?* That little bastard—"

"No," I said. "I talked with him and I'm satisfied it wasn't him. But his name should have been on this list. Stop thinking like an aristocrat, Rembek, and give me a complete list."

There were three or four seconds of dead silence, and then he said, "You're right. Chesterton used that, in the story about the mailman, what's the title?"

"I wouldn't know," I said.

He said, "I read it years ago. Now, what was the title? See, that's going to drive me crazy now. The point of the story was, you don't see people that are part of the background. Like everybody made up lists of the people that were there, and nobody thought to put the mailman on the list, and naturally it was the mailman that did it."

"That's what I want," I said. "All the mailmen."

"Let me think some more," he said. "If there's anybody else I left out, I'll send you over a revised list. You want anything else?"

"Yes. I want a legman, somebody to run the office for me."

"You want a gopher. Check. You'll have one there within half an hour. What else?"

"Have you got a copy of this list?"

"Naturally."

"All right. Send some men out to get the alibis for the night before last. The killer could have made the round trip to Allentown and back in about three hours, and he could have arrived out there any time between eleven-thirty Wednesday night and, say, seven Thursday morning. Since she'd just taken a shower, it was probably not very much after midnight."

"She just took a shower? Before she was killed? I didn't know about that."

He was silent, and I knew he was feeling the bite of specific memories. Remembering that apartment, the small green tubless bathroom and the crowded bedroom with the patchwork quilt on the bed, I could visualize approximations of the memories that had their teeth in his neck, but only to an extent; I had never seen Rita Castle's face.

I said, "An alibi is a story that leaves no three-hour openings between ten o'clock Wednesday night and eight-thirty Thursday morning."

"Right," he said. His voice was strange. He cleared his throat and said, in his normal voice, "I'll try and get it for you sometime this afternoon. You going to be in the office?"

"Yes. Until I get the answer on the alibis. Then I'll want to interview the ones that are left."

"Check. What else?"

"A picture of Rita Castle. More than one, if possible, different shots."

"No problem. What else?"

"Did she ever introduce you to friends of hers from before she met you?"

"What, that Village crowd? No, she knew better."

"Never? Not one?"

"Not one."

That was just as well. In the note, she'd said, "I have found a real man," and that read as though she meant a man she'd met subsequent to meeting Rembek. But I'd wanted to check out the other possibility anyway. This way I was saved some work.

I said, "When you're sending over new lists, include Dominic Brono's address and phone number."

"You *do* think it was him."

"No, I don't. I'm a completist."

"Is that straight?"

"Rembek, I'll tell you when I suspect somebody."

"All right. What else?"

"You said you'd get me the police lab report."

"It's on its way to New York right now, you should have it within the hour."

"Good."

"You want me to make the appointments for you to talk to these guys?"

"Our suspects? No, wait till the preliminary check is done."

"Right. What else?"

"Nothing at the moment."

"Good. May I say something, Mister Tobin?"

"Go ahead."

"I believe the Police Department made a mistake."

We hung up then, and I went to work at the electric typewriter, making a preliminary report, putting down a summary of everything that had happened so far. I broke off in the middle of it when I remembered to call Kate. I phoned her, gave her the number here, told her I didn't know when I'd be home, and went back to the report.

I was finishing up when there was a knock at the door. When I called "Come in," the door opened and my gopher entered.

71

It was funny; he *looked* like a gopher, small and brown and nervous, with the shaky actions of a sporadic drunk. He told me his name was Mickey Hansel, and I told him I wanted him to go out and buy some things. He looked alert.

"A box of file folders," I said, "to fit that cabinet there." I took my notebook from my pocket. "Two notebooks like this. And coffee and Danish for both of us."

"Yes, sir," he said. "File folders. Notebooks. Coffee and Danish."

"And tell the elevator operator we'll want a worktable in here for you."

"Yes, sir, will do." He gave me a nervous half-salute and a nervous half-smile and went away again.

The worktable came in before my gopher came back. (You understand, they're called gophers because they go for things.) Two men in undershirts carried the table in and set it in the corner and went out again. It was a rectangular wooden table, as old and beaten and scarred as my desk.

When Mickey Hansel came back, I said, "What do you know about what's going on?"

Promptly he said, "Not a thing, sir."

"Oh, come on, they must have told you *something* when they sent you over here."

"Yes, sir. They give me the address, they said you was an ex-cop and still square but you was doing a job for Mister Rembek and I should do whatever you wanted."

"The first thing I want," I said, "is for you to know the story. A man works better when he knows what the job is all about."

He looked unconvinced, but he said, "Yes, sir."

I gave him the report I'd just finished. He pulled the chair over to his worktable, sat down, and read it slowly and carefully, moving his lips and making sibilant sounds on the esses.

72

While waiting for him to be done, I stood at the window and watched Fifth Avenue.

When he finished he put the report back on my desk and said, "Yes, sir. I'm done."

"You've got the picture now?"

"Yes, sir. That's a real shame about that Miss Castle, she was an awful good-lookin girl."

"You knew her?"

"Sometimes Mister Rembek would have me bring stuff up to her place. You know, presents and all."

That was good. Now I had a control for Rembek's revised list. If Mickey Hansel's name didn't show up on it, I'd know Rembek still wasn't thinking right. Not that there was much chance Mickey was Rita Castle's "real man." But I'd asked for a complete list, wanting the right to make my own decision about who should be considered and who not, and a complete list would have to include Mickey Hansel.

Now I asked Mickey if he had any questions about what he'd read, and when he said he didn't, he thought he understood what was going on, I put him to work making up file folders for each of the ten names on Rembek's first list. Eleven, including Dominic Brono.

While Mickey was working on that, a kid in a leather jacket brought me a bulky manila envelope containing photocopies of the medical and lab and police reports from Allentown. I sat down and read them while Mickey laboriously printed names on folder tabs.

Rita Castle had been killed sometime between midnight and three A.M. on Thursday morning, struck down by a single blow on the back of the head. The blow had been struck with a great deal of force, fracturing the skull. Microscopic bits of metal in the wound, plus the violence of the impact, led police to suspect the weapon had been a hammer or some similar tool. No trace of the weapon had been found.

There were no witnesses to the arrival or departure of the killer, who had presumably used an automobile but who might have left it parked a distance away and come on foot. There were no significant usable fingerprints on anything. Rita Castle had no known contacts or acquaintances in the Allentown-Bethlehem area. The pale blue Ford Mustang parked outside her motel room was registered to her in the state and city of New York. The rest was material I already knew.

While I was still reading these reports, another messenger arrived, this one bringing a manila envelope containing photos of Rita Castle. There were four photos, all eight-by-eleven glossies, each with a mimeographed résumé of her acting credits pasted to the back. One showed her looking soulful in a white gown, with misty lighting and a shadowy background. Another had her looking healthy and girl-next-door, smiling directly at the camera, wearing a bulky sweater, with trees and foliage in the background. The third, with a dead-white background, showed her in a stylish black dress and a strand of pearls, looking perkily over her shoulder, a somewhat arch smile of pixie good humor on her face. The fourth was a composite, four photos spaced around the available area, showing her demonstrating a variety of expressions, all while wearing a man's white shirt and sitting on a modernistic sofa.

She had been quite a beautiful girl but very much of a type. One connects that kind of good looks with television commercials set in ski lodges. In two of the photos I saw very clearly the "dumb bunny" that Roger Kerrigan had described, but in the other pictures too much brain showed behind the eyes. This had been a smart and clever and capable girl, self-assured and unworried.

Why had such a girl chosen to take off like that in the first place? It seemed very much out of character. I decided I would have to ask the man when I found him.

About four o'clock Rembek called me. "I've got the new list," he said.

"Good."

"I've also got the rundown on the first ten. Three of them are clear, they got alibis there's no question on. What do we do about the rest now?"

I said, "There's a chance we can eliminate some more. This medical report here narrows the time down. Any one of those people who can prove he was in town during the half-hour period around one-thirty Thursday morning is in the clear."

"How come?"

"It takes a minimum of an hour and a half to get to Allentown from here. She was killed between twelve and three. That means, if she was killed at the earliest possible time, midnight, the killer couldn't have gotten back to the city before one-thirty. And if she was killed at the latest possible time, three o'clock, he couldn't have *left* New York any later than one-thirty."

"Okay, hold on, I've got it all written down here." There was silence a while, and when he came back he said, "Two more down. Five left."

"Plus the second list. How many on that?"

"Six. I feel like an idiot, Mister Tobin, making a mistake like that. It just goes to show the way the mind works. I've already got them being checked out the same way."

"Good. Now will you set up interviews for me with the five left from the first list?"

"Will do. For today?"

"If possible."

"It's possible, Mister Tobin. Whatever you want is possible."

"Good. Is Roger Kerrigan one of the five left?"

"Right. He had no alibi at all. You don't think it was him, do you?"

"No. But I won't need to talk to him tonight."

"Uh, well, that's the thing, Mister Tobin. He'll have to be along with you when you make the interviews. The, uh, the people in charge want to know what's going on. You know, what questions you're asking, and like that."

"That's all right," I said. "I don't mind him being around."

"Fine. I'm glad to hear it."

I said, "There's a Canfield on this list, too. Isn't that the attorney I met at your place?"

"Right. Eustace Canfield. He's out, definitely out."

"All right. You say you have all the reports on paper?"

"You want them?"

"Yes. I want to keep all the material in one place, for easy reference."

"Right. I'll send it over now. And I'll let you know about the interviews."

"Thank you."

I hung up. Mickey Hansel was standing beside the desk, looking at the pictures of Rita Castle. "You know," he said, shaking his head, looking at the pictures, "it's a real shame."

"Her being killed like that," I said. "Yes, I guess it is."

"Oh, yeah, that, too," he said.

"Why? What did you mean?"

"I meant me," he said. "What a bum I am." He shook his head, looking at the pictures. "The best day I lived," he said, "I couldn't have had a piece of that. The best day I lived."

11

At five o'clock I sent Mickey home with the spare office key and instructions to come in at nine in the morning, do whatever filing I might leave for him, take any phone messages that might come in, and wait for further word from me.

Now I was alone, with the day beginning to darken outside the windows behind me, and I felt myself stopping, descending to a halt, as though someone had taken their foot off the accelerator. So long as there was another person around—even Mickey—I could go through the motions with no trouble, but once I was alone the truth inescapably emerged, causing me to slump at the desk like an unused marionette. I had no real interest in what I was doing, no real interest in anything. I spent the time thinking about my wall.

Roger Kerrigan showed up at twenty after five, with a briefcase. From it he took the alibi reports and Rita Castle's note and the new list, and his presence made me active again. I checked the list and saw that Mickey Hansel was there, next to the bottom. Also William Pietrojetti, the accountant. I wrote a note to Mickey to make up folders on these names— "except yourself"—clipped the note to the list, and put it on Mickey's worktable.

Kerrigan, grinning, said, "You run this like a little business."

"It is a business," I said. "What about the interviews?"

"They're all set up for this evening, forty-five minutes

apart. Is that time enough?"

"More than enough."

"They'll be at Ernie's place."

"That's no good," I said. "I want to see each of them at home."

He frowned. "Does it make a difference?"

"Yes."

"Let me use your phone, then."

I got up from the desk and he called Rembek and made the change. While he was on the phone I sat at the worktable and started going over the alibi reports, looking at the eliminations first. They all looked good.

When he hung up, Kerrigan said to me, "Done. And those other six'll be checked out by tomorrow morning."

"Good."

He said, "I'm one of the possibles, right?"

"So far."

"Then you can interview me while we have dinner. Your first appointment isn't till seven-thirty."

"All right. Let me check this stuff first."

I now looked at the reports on the five who were still suspect, starting with Kerrigan himself, who claimed to have been home alone Wednesday night, watching television, first the Tonight Show and then a Boris Karloff-Bela Lugosi horror movie called *The Black Cat*. Since the Tonight Show ended at one, he could have left after it and still made Allentown in time. And since *The Black Cat* was a movie made in 1935, Kerrigan's knowledge of its plot did not necessarily mean he had watched it Wednesday night.

Next on the list was a man named Frank Donner, whose occupation was listed as "businessman (vending machines)," who claimed to have spent a quiet evening with his wife and to have gone to bed at eleven-thirty. He and his wife had separate bedrooms, but we wouldn't have taken her unsupported word for it anyway.

Next was Louis Hogan, occupation union official, who had driven back to New York Wednesday night from Washington, arriving home at two-thirty in the morning. Allentown would not have been too much of a detour for him to make.

Then Joseph Lydon, occupation realtor, who claimed to have been with his mistress from eight-thirty Wednesday evening till two-fifteen Thursday morning, in her apartment. She was hardly a witness whose unsubstantiated word could count for much.

And finally Paul Einhorn, occupation airline executive, who claimed to have been pub-crawling by himself Wednesday night and who didn't know exactly what time he'd gotten home except that it was after the bars closed.

The last thing I looked at was Rita Castle's note. The wording certainly had that dumb-bunny effect Roger Kerrigan had mentioned and which I had seen in two of the photos of Rita Castle that Rembek had sent over:

> I am going away. I have found a real man and we are going to find a new life together far away. You'll never see either of us again.

We were making certain assumptions based on the particular wording of that note. We were assuming the man involved was—for Rita Castle, at any rate—a potent lover, or at least more potent than Ernie Rembek. We were assuming he was someone Rembek knew. There didn't seem to be any reason not to make these assumptions, and to stay with them until and unless they led us into a blind alley. If that happened, we would have to abandon them and start again with a new set of assumptions.

What would that new set of assumptions be? I studied the note, trying to see other ways to read it, and drew a complete blank.

Well. Time enough for that if and when we ever got to that blind alley. I put the note away in the filing cabinet, left the alibi reports on the worktable for Mickey to file, and cleared papers and pencils from my desk into the center drawer. Then I shrugged into my coat, and Kerrigan and I left the office and went downstairs to the street. We got a cab, with some difficulty, and went uptown to a very expensive restaurant, named by Kerrigan. When I said something about the price, Kerrigan said, "Forget it, businessman. You're on an expense account, remember?"

The food wasn't worth the price, but then again it couldn't have been. We didn't talk until we were on the coffee, and then Kerrigan said, "Now you want to ask me questions."

"I might as well," I said, "since I've got you here." I took a new notebook from my pocket, flipped it open on the table, got out my pen. "Your name is Roger Kerrigan. Was it always?"

He cocked a half-smile. "Always," he said.

"Middle name?"

"Oscar. After my grandfather."

"Age?"

"Thirty-four."

"On my list it gives your job as co-ordinator. What does that mean?"

"This part you shouldn't write down," he said.

"All right." I put down the pen and picked up my coffee cup.

He said, "The corporation has a certain area, mostly the Northeast, down as far as Washington, west as far as Ohio. Then there's districts, and each district runs itself. Like Ernie Rembek, he runs this district, he never gets any orders from the corporation or anything like that. But sometimes things happen, there's this kind of trouble, that kind of trouble, and the corporation has to find out if things are okay in the district. So that's my job."

"The corporation sends you in to look around?"

"Not exactly. I'm here all the time. I live in New York, I know Ernie socially. It's just every once in a while I get a call, the corporation wants to know what's going on with such-and-such. Or sometimes Ernie wants to pass the word about something to the corporation, and then he comes to me."

"You're what they used to call a troubleshooter."

"Something like that."

"But the corporation doesn't send you into any other districts. This is the only one you worry about."

"Oh, no. I'm the co-ordinator for all New York City and Long Island and Westchester."

"That's a lot of different districts."

"Nine," he said.

"And you know all the other district leaders socially, too? The way you know Ernie Rembek?"

"Sure, more or less. Ernie I know best, because I live right here in his district. Also, we get along on a personal basis. There's a guy out in Nassau County, for instance, in a personal way I can't stand him, so I never go out there unless I have to."

I said, "How long have you had this job?"

"Five—no, six years."

"How did you get it?"

He grinned. "By being sharp."

"What did you do before this?"

"You don't want my whole history, Mister Tobin."

"Yes, I do."

"Well, you're not going to get it."

81

"All right. Have you got a record?"

"No."

"No arrests?"

"Not civilian."

"What's that mean?"

He'd suddenly lost his urbanity. "It means I did stockade time in the Army when I was a baby, all right?"

"How much of a baby?"

"Nineteen. I did six months."

It was an injustice—real or imagined—that obviously still inflamed him. I let it go, saying, "Are you married?"

"No. Divorced."

"How long ago?"

This subject left him in better humor. Making his crooked smile, he said, "You want that history, too? At the age of twenty-two I married a girl I'd met in night school. The marriage lasted six years, and now the divorce has lasted six years. I'd put my money on the divorce, if I were you."

"You went to night school?"

"I had the idea I'd be a lawyer. But I make a bad student."

"Do you still see your ex-wife?"

"No."

"Why not?"

"Beverly's a social worker. I don't hang out in that kind of neighborhood."

"Would you say it would be accurate to call you cynical?"

With a cynical smile he said, "Not exactly. I like to call myself a realist. I know what's happening."

"How long have you known Ernie Rembek?"

"Nine years."

"Socially?"

"No. That would be about six years. As long as I've been co-ordinator. Before that I was too far down the ladder. The movers and shakers don't socialize with the hired help."

"How long have you known Rita Castle?"

"Since Ernie bought her."

"Bought? That's a strange verb."

"No, it isn't. It's the only verb that fits."

"You didn't like Rita Castle."

He shrugged. "We already talked about her. *She* was what you'd call cynical."

"You made a pass at her?"

His crooked grin flashed again. "Let's say I made a shoe-string catch of one of hers."

"What happened?"

"She called interference."

"What does that mean?"

"It means she liked to tease herself behind Ernie's back, setting things up that she *could* do and then not doing them."

"How badly did she burn you?"

"Slight singe of the fingertips. I try to take care of myself, and one of the ways to do it is stay away from trouble like that."

"Did you ever warn Rembek about her?"

He shook his head. "When a man buys something new and shiny, and he loves it very much, you don't tell him he got a lemon."

"Do you know of anybody else she threw passes at?"

"Not from knowledge, no. I would guess she threw a lot of them."

"Nobody ever talked to you about her."

"No."

"There was no rumor about her and anybody else."

"Not that I ever heard."

"All right." I put notebook and pen away, and finished my coffee. "Is it time for our first interview?"

"You mean second interview." He looked at his watch. "Right. Time to go see Frank Donner."

He signed the check, and we left.

12

Frank Donner lived in an old co-op apartment building in Washington Heights. From his windows could be seen the graceful arc of the lights of the George Washington Bridge, and the dark river, and the scattered lights of New Jersey. The building itself had lost some of its original elegance, but the Donner apartment was unchanged, a museum to the memory of 1935. The colors were dark, the draperies were massive, the corners were rounded. Amber mirrors glowed darkly from unexpected places, the light sources were many but were individually dim, and the carpet that flowed everywhere, from room to room, from color scheme to color scheme, was a uniform purple, as though there'd been a flood in a wine factory.

Frank Donner himself, fifty-five and gone to fat, looked almost like a banker or a prosperous businessman, complete to the dark suit and the expensive cigar, but a certain toughness around the eyes and looseness around the mouth gave him away; he was a thug who had made good.

His wife, who welcomed us to the living room, was an astonishingly stout woman, actually ugly with fat, wearing a bright-colored flowered dress that merely emphasized the breadth of her. In her smile when she greeted us could be seen the faint echo of the girl she had been, always a bit on the plump side but once pleasant to look upon.

Kerrigan and Donner shook hands, greeting each other with a formality that Donner obviously found natural and that Kerrigan tolerated, and then Kerrigan introduced me, and Donner gravely shook my hand, too, which I gave him after only the smallest hesitation. Donner introduced me to his wife, giving her name as Ethel, and then we all sat down, including Ethel.

I said to Donner, "I'd prefer to talk just to you."

"Ethel knows my entire life," Donner assured me. "Everything in business I tell her, talk over with her."

"I'd still prefer to talk just to you."

Donner's wife beamed at me, full of good will, saying, "I won't interrupt a thing, Mister Tobin, that's a promise."

I looked at Kerrigan who said to Donner, "Frank, I think Ernie wants us to co-operate with Mister Tobin."

Donner's heavy face took on a mulish look. "I've never had nothing behind Ethel's back in twenty-eight years of marriage. I don't see no reason I should start now."

I got to my feet. "I'll talk to you some other time," I said, and started for the door.

Kerrigan caught up with me in the vestibule. "Hold it a second," he said. "Let me talk to him. You wait out here."

I said, "I want the answers he'll give when she's not listening."

"I know what you want," he said, "and you're right. Except with Frank, believe me the answers won't be any different."

"When I ask him to describe the girl, what he thought of her?"

"Maybe," he conceded. "Let me talk to them for a minute."

I waited under the chandelier, seeing myself reflected in amber mirrors. What were all these people to me, why should I concern myself with the labyrinths of their minds? I had my own labyrinth to contend with. I had a wall to build. The door was beside me, but I didn't quite leave.

After a couple of minutes Kerrigan came back, nodding and saying, "It's okay."

I went back into the living room and Donner was alone in there now, but still looking mulish. He was going to give me a bad time, make it tough for me to do a job I didn't want to do in the first place, and I disliked him for it. I stood in front of him and said, "If you and your wife are inseparable, how come you've got separate bedrooms?"

He flared up immediately, coming up out of the seat, red-faced and glaring, and then caught control of himself midway, sank back again, opened his fists, looked over at Kerrigan, and still red-faced said, "I got to put up with this?"

I said, "Donner, what we're looking for is the guy who stole Ernie Rembek's woman and then killed her. You've got a bad alibi. You spend all your time pushing the idea of how devoted you are to your wife, but my report says you and she have separate bedrooms. That looks to me like a contradiction. It even looks to me like you might be trying to build up the faithful-husband image just to distract people from the notion that you were playing around with Rita Castle on the side."

"I never once looked at another woman," he said hotly. "In twenty-eight years of marriage, not *once* did I look at another woman."

"Not till Rita Castle."

"Do you—" But then he stopped, abruptly, and the anger faded from his face, and he looked at Kerrigan and said, "You didn't have to tell me he used to be a cop. That's the way they all act."

I said, "Why not talk to me, Donner!"

"Sure," he said. He sat back in the sofa, ostentatiously relaxed, behaving now as he would if hauled into the station for

87

questioning, sitting there smug and sure of himself, waiting for the inevitable lawyer to come take him away. "Go ahead," he said. "Ask away."

"I will." I went back to my chair and sat down. I took my notebook and pen out and said, "When did you first meet Rita Castle?"

He said, "You gonna take notes?"

Amused, Kerrigan told him, "That's the way he does things, Frank. Everything businesslike. You should see the office we gave him, everything in files, reports all typed up, it looks like the Motor Vehicle Bureau."

I said to Donner, "Will it bother you if I take notes?"

He shrugged, saying, "Naw, I was just surprised is all."

I poised pen over notebook and said, "When did you first meet Rita Castle?"

This time he answered me, saying, "I don't know, exactly. A little while after Ernie started going with her."

"What were the circumstances of that first meeting, do you remember?"

"Sure. I met her at a party."

"Where was this party?"

"Here." He looked at Kerrigan. "You were here," he said.

I said, "Rembek brought Rita Castle to this party instead of his wife? What did Mrs. Donner think about that?"

He said, "The Rembeks have had their share of troubles, I don't know how much you know about that. Eleanor's my sister, you know."

"That's Mrs. Rembek?"

He nodded. "That's right. Eleanor is a wonderful woman, anybody'll tell you that, but she's got problems, had them since she was a kid. Nerves. She's a very delicate lady. She don't go out to parties at all any more. My wife and I, we both know the situation, we know Ernie's devoted to Eleanor, and we understand the situation he's in. So he has a young woman and he takes her to parties, we're all couples, you know, some married couples and some like Roger here that bring a date, and a man without a woman wouldn't fit in, you know what I mean? Some of the wives in our crowd wouldn't invite Ernie at all if he'd come by himself."

I said, "What did you think of Rita Castle?"

"She was a very pretty lady."

"That's all?"

He said, "My wife could maybe give you a better impression, she talked to her more than I did. You know how it is at parties, the men wind up in the kitchen talking cars and football, the women wind up in the living room talking God knows what."

I said, "Thank you. Could I speak to your wife for a minute?"

He chuckled and said, "Alone?"

"Yes," I said, which surprised him. I turned away from his surprise and said to Kerrigan. "Without you, too."

Donner seemed about ready to get outraged again, but I let Kerrigan talk to him and ultimately they left the room and sent Mrs. Donner in. She came in with a hesitant smile on her face, her hands clasped in front of her, saying, "Did you want to speak to me?"

"Yes, I did. In the first place, I want to apologize for my rudeness earlier, but I didn't have any choice."

She accepted that graciously, thanking me, and then I said, "Now I'm going to have to be ill-mannered again, and this time I'll apologize in advance."

She waited, seeming to brace herself but saying nothing.

"I'm about ready," I said, "to cross your husband's name off my list of suspects. You do know the case I'm on, don't you?"

"The death of Miss Castle," she said.

"Yes. There's only one question left in my mind about your husband, and he refuses to answer it. I'm hoping you will."

"I will if I can," she said.

"Your husband," I said, "gives every indication of preferring to be with you at all times, and if this is true, then obviously he isn't the man I'm looking for. But if it is false, if it's simply make-believe, then very likely he is the man I'm looking for."

"It isn't false, Mister Tobin," she said. "My husband and I are truly very close."

"But there's one contradiction, Mrs. Donner, and your husband won't explain it."

"A contradiction?"

"According to my report, you and your husband have separate bedrooms."

She blushed, very red. "Oh," she said, her flustered hands going to her red face. "Oh, I see."

"If you could tell me—"

"Oh, I imagine he got very angry when you asked him that," she said.

"As a matter of fact, he did."

"Yes." She hesitated, still blushing, still flustered, and then, all in a rush, she said, "The reason for it is, the reason for it is, it seems I snore!"

"Oh," I said.

"Oh, it's really awful," she said, babbling on to cover her embarrassment. "Sometimes it's so bad I wake myself up. We even had my room soundproofed. I've been to doctors and they say there just isn't anything to be done about it, not a thing."

"I'm sorry, Mrs. Donner," I said. "I apologize for having

to ask the question."

"Oh, no, not at all, not at all. I can see why it didn't make sense to you, why you had to know."

"Thank you," I said. "You are very gracious."

We went out to the vestibule, where Donner and Kerrigan were waiting for us. Donner began at once to stare at his wife as though looking for some sign of abuse, but she smiled reassuringly at him and made a production of shaking my hand and thanking me for coming and apologizing for not having given me anything to eat or drink. Donner relaxed a little after that, and even seemed to want to end the interview on a rising note of friendship, which I resisted. His wife had captured me—against incredible odds, it seemed to me—but Donner was still to me no more than a hood I had met in the course of an unpleasant job. I took his outstretched hand reluctantly, and left as rapidly as possible.

Outside, as we waited for the elevator, Kerrigan said to me, grinning, "Well, did you find out?"

"Yes."

"Nothing bad, I hope."

"Nothing bad." I felt I owed Mrs. Donner at least my silence.

The elevator came then, and we got aboard. Riding down, I said, "Is Donner just a brother-in-law of Rembek's, or a business associate?"

Kerrigan said, "Business associate."

"Doing what?"

"He handles distribution on machines. Gambling."

"Is there still much of that in New York? I never ran into it."

"Every American Legion post has its slot machines," he said, "and over in Brooklyn there's more pinball machines than people. And there's still a couple large rooms in

91

Manhattan." He shook his head at me, grinning. "A cop wouldn't hear about them," he said. "Not down at your level."

I said, "Is he the same Frank Donner used to be a strong-arm boy for the Lako brothers?"

"That was years ago."

"He hasn't changed much."

Kerrigan raised an eyebrow, disagreeing gently. He said, "You crossing him off the list?"

Why was my mind listing dissimilarities between Rita Castle and Linda Campbell? Why did I want to go on thinking that Frank Donner might be the man who had run away with Rita Castle?

"No," I said. "We'll leave him on awhile."

13

In the next cab, Kerrigan filled me in on Louis Hogan, number two on my list. Hogan was a national delegate in the Amalgamated Refrigeration Workers Union, but had at one time been directly a member of what Kerrigan insisted on calling the "corporation," by which he meant the mob. The ARWU was not associated with the corporation in any primary way, but some legitimate sideline businesses that corporation members—like Ernie Rembek—were involved in did involve an association with the ARWU and other unions, and Louis Hogan was in the position of being able from time to time to do his former associates favors. These favors were always suitably rewarded.

Judging by where he lived, the rewards were lavish. In the upper Bronx there is a residential section of great beauty and exclusivity, with large private homes widely separated along curving tree-shaded streets, an area of low hills and many fir trees, where most of the houses are hidden from their neighbors and many boast—though they wouldn't actually boast—swimming pools. It was in a stone-and-siding house in this area that Louis Hogan lived.

The cab let us out at the foot of the blacktop driveway, which led uphill on an easy curve past a rock garden to the house, which could be just barely seen from the road. Kerrigan and I walked up the curving blacktop and then off it onto a slate path across the lawn to the shrubbery-flanked front door. Kerrigan rang, and after a minute we were admitted by a Negro maid in black dress, white apron, and little white cap. Kerrigan gave our names, she ushered us in to the living room, and there we waited while she went to tell Hogan we were here.

The living room was long, with a fireplace at the far end and a picture window facing the lawn. Several sofas were the room's main furniture, one facing the picture window, one facing the fireplace, and one at this end facing a television-phonograph console. I went close to the only painting on the wall, opposite the window, and saw that it was an original rather than a print, an abstraction which ran heavily to blues. I couldn't make out the name of the artist, in the lower right corner.

There was a string quartet playing somewhere in the house, just at the threshold of audibility. A large and beautiful boxer dog came padding into the room and studied us calmly and with no particular interest. As Louis Hogan entered, the dog padded out again.

Louis Hogan was about forty, possibly a few years older, but kept himself in shape, probably with a gym in the basement. His hair, black turning gray in the combination called pepper-and-salt, was in a brushlike crewcut above a square, bony, strong-looking face. He exuded a sort of after-shave manliness and probably drove an American sports car. He shook my hand in a forthright way, offered us drinks, which we both refused, and urged us to sit down and make ourselves comfortable.

When we were all seated, I began my questioning with, "I understand your association with Ernie Rembek these days is more or less just social. That is, you yourself aren't in the rackets any more."

"Right," he said briskly. "Not that I was ever exactly what you might call in the rackets. You take a look for a record on me, my friend, and you'll find nothing there."

I said, "In that case, I suppose you met Rita Castle first at some sort of social function."

"Right. One of Frank Donner's parties." He looked at Kerrigan. "You were there."

I said to Kerrigan, "Same party?"

"Yes," he said. "That was the first time Ernie took Rita anywhere." He explained to Hogan, "We just came from Frank's place."

Hogan seemed amused and surprised, saying, "*He's* a suspect?"

I said, "You don't think he should be?"

"God, no!"

"Do you think you make a more sensible suspect?"

"Much," he said, with the same briskness.

The answer surprised me, and I was conscious of Kerrigan grinning at me. I said to Hogan, "Why do you think that?"

He said, "Because I'm capable of the kind of relationship with a woman that the killer apparently had with Rita Castle. I've kept myself in shape. I'm still interested in women, and women are still interested in me."

"In other words, you're a real man."

"That's comic-book phrasing, but the idea's about right."

Kerrigan said to me, "The wording of the note hasn't been spread around."

"Good," I said.

Hogan looked from one of us to the other. "Something?"

"Nothing important," I said. "*Did* you have a relationship with Rita Castle?"

"Yes," he said.

"You did? What was it?"

"The third or fourth time I met her was here in this house. We had a party and Ernie brought her. It was in the summer.

95

Out by the pool she started one of those come-get-me routines with me, the kind you can spot it's a phony a mile away. I ignored her and she kept it up. We've got a freezer out in the garage, and when I went out to get more ice cubes she came after me, so I put her down on the floor and . . . rubbed her a little. You might say I gave her an inspection. Then I told her what I was to Ernie and what she was to Ernie and I said she shouldn't play any more games in my house, not with me or anybody else, and I let her go."

"What did she do?"

He shrugged. "She came in here and sat down. On the sofa there. And stayed there till Ernie took her home."

"Nothing happened after that?"

He shook his head. "Nothing. I guess she never said anything to Ernie. She never tried anything with me again, and never tried anything with anybody else when I was around, but I heard she did act up sometimes same as before."

"What was her attitude toward you?"

"Distant," he said, and shrugged again. "We wouldn't have had much to say anyway."

"Did you tell your wife about what happened in the garage?"

"No. There wasn't any point."

"If you had judged Rita Castle's invitation to be real, would you have taken her up on it?"

He considered, and said, "I'm not sure. Possibly. Ernie and I have been friends for years, but this would be a special case. It would depend on other things, I guess."

"What other things?"

"Like what my personal life was like at the time."

"You mean, whether or not you already had someone?"

"That's part of it."

"Do you have someone now?"

He glanced over his shoulder at the doorway, which remained empty, and said, "Yes."

"Could I have her name and address?"

"She lives in Washington," he said.

"That's all right."

"She's married."

"Then I'll use discretion."

Reluctantly he gave me the name and address. When I asked him who might verify this relationship, he even more reluctantly gave me the name of a motel owner in Chevy Chase, a man who was a personal friend of the woman involved and more recently a personal friend of Hogan's.

After writing it all down, I said, "I take it this is where you left from Wednesday night."

"Right."

"And these two people will verify the time of your leaving."

"If it's necessary," he said coldly.

"It may not be," I said. "Is Mrs. Hogan at home?"

"No, she's at a meeting." He cocked his head toward the sound of chamber music and said, "My daughter. Fifteen years old. They talk about the kind of music kids listen to, but they forget there's all kinds of kids." He showed his first smile since coming in here, a display of parental pride, and said, "Isn't that something? Picked it up by herself. I've got a tin ear."

I got to my feet. "Thank you," I said. "I guess that's all I need for now."

"Glad to help," he said, rising. "If you'll just try to be a little cautious how you ask questions in Washington . . ."

I promised I would be extremely cautious, and we left.

14

We crossed the Triborough Bridge into Queens and headed east, sitting in the back of yet another cab. Our next interview was to be with a man named Joseph Lydon, occupation realtor, who lived in a high-rise apartment building in the Corona section of Queens, not far from the 108th Street exit of the Long Island Expressway.

On the way, Kerrigan told me something about Lydon, the son of a now-dead former associate of Ernie Rembek's. The father, Ralph Lydon, had turned his profits from the corporation into real estate, eventually building up a large realty concern, with properties of various kinds in Queens and Brooklyn, ranging from luxury apartment buildings like the one in which Joseph Lydon now lived to slum tenements in areas like Bushwick. Like Louis Hogan, Joseph Lydon's association with Ernie Rembek was now mostly social, although for a realtor, too, there were those occasions when one could use the help of the corporation or offer help of one's own. A number of corporation businesses leased properties from Joseph Lydon's firm, and there were other links between them.

The apartment building, when we got to it, proved to be one of the mammoth new city-within-a-city affairs, three different buildings rising up like brick Ritz Cracker boxes on the same broad landscaped plot of land, with playgrounds and a first-floor nursery school, underground garages, a supermarket on the premises, and a synagogue and chapel in the basements.

Lydon lived in the top-floor penthouse of the main building. We rang the bell downstairs and closed-circuit television showed our faces to the man who answered in the Lydon apartment. His metallic voice came from the grid to our left, asking us who we were. We identified ourselves, the voice told us someone would be right down to get us and bring us up, and the front door buzzed to let us in.

I soon found out why we had to be escorted from the lobby; the elevator had no button to push for the penthouse floor. Instead, there was a keyhole above the line of buttons, discreetly marked PH. Putting the right key in it and making a half-turn sent the elevator up to the top.

The man who came down to get us was short, graying, stooped, and diffident, acting toward us as though our recommendations would either keep him his job or cost it, and as though he'd been warned that our grading was usually severe. He bowed and scraped us into the elevator, turned the key, pocketed it, and faced front in nervous silence all the way up, seeming to wish he could somehow become invisible, thereby being even more inoffensive.

At the top, the elevator opened onto a red-carpeted foyer, discreetly furnished, across which our guide discreetly led us and through an archway into a large long living room dominated by its windows.

I suppose the best thing to say for the view was that it was comprehensive. From here one could see a long way out across Queens, with the raw ground of new apartment building construction close to hand, the gray scar of the Long Island Expressway in the middle distance, and the squat seedy houses of Queens—one- and two-family, packed in nearly wall to wall—stretching away toward the horizon like a cruel parody of Faust's dream. Knowing that I too lived out there somewhere, even though too far away to be seen from here, made me suddenly embarrassed and uneasy in a way I had never known before. I turned away quickly from the view and concentrated my attention on the man who owned it.

Joseph Lydon was about thirty, short and a bit stocky, expensively dressed, holding a drink in one hand and affecting an air of easy negligence that I found particularly irritating. He had the pudgy cheeks and petulant mouth of a man who began life as a spoiled brat and had never been given any reason to change. His eyes had the snotty quality one sees in those undergraduate collegians who instigate trouble that others will eventually be caught for.

He said to me, "Ernie Rembek told me about you. You're the first ex-cop I ever saw. Is it like being a defrocked priest?" He hadn't greeted Kerrigan at all, and didn't offer either of us a drink.

I sat down, unasked, crossed my legs, and said, "When was the first time you met Rita Castle?"

"Well, well," he said, "no wasted motion with you, eh? Right to the point."

"I don't have a great deal of time to spare with you," I said.

"Then we must hurry right along," he said, and sat down facing me. "What was the question again?"

"When was the first time you met Rita Castle?"

"Let me see—" He appeared to think. "About three weeks ago," he said.

I looked at Kerrigan, and back at Lydon. "Three weeks ago? That was the first time you ever met Rita Castle?"

"Oh, *first* time! I thought you said *last* time!" He seemed to think his mistake was funny.

"If you'll listen to me carefully, Lydon," I said, "we'll be able to do this faster."

"I'm sure you're right," he said, and allowed the mask of general snottiness to slip long enough to show me I'd gotten to him. He didn't like me at all, and that was very good. He said, "The first time I met Rita was, I suppose, a year and a half ago."

"Where?"

"Here. Ernie brought her to a little party here."

I glanced at Kerrigan. "He wasn't at the famous Donner party?"

It was Lydon himself who answered, saying with a laugh, "Frank Donner? Go to one of those wakes at *his* place? Thank you, but no thank you."

"You weren't invited or you just didn't go?"

"Frank Donner and I seldom see one another. We don't have much in common."

"What about this last time you saw Rita Castle? Three weeks ago, you said? Where was that?"

"At her place. There was a show that some of us had money in, we went to the opening night, Ernie gave a little private party afterwards at her apartment."

"Who else was there?"

He shrugged. "A few of the regulars. Lou Hogan and Fritz Kenn and Jack Harper and Eustace Canfield, maybe a couple more."

Kenn and Harper were names with alibis from the original list, and so was Canfield, the attorney. I said, "Were you mostly with women?"

He laughed sardonically. "Are you kidding? I said it was the theater, an opening night. It was wifey time. Even Lou brought his beast along."

"You're married, aren't you?"

His smile got more bitter. "You mean it shows?"

"On the report," I told him, "it said you spent Wednesday

night with your mistress. Single men don't usually speak of their women friends as mistresses."

"Elementary, my dear Watson!" he said mockingly, and turned to Kerrigan, saying, "You see? Ernie's hired a regular Sherlock Holmes!"

I said, "Is your wife here?"

"No," he said bluntly. "I don't know where she is. I never do. If you want to talk to her, I'll leave her a note. She may get in touch with you or she may not."

"That won't be necessary," I said. "At least, not right now. What was your opinion of Rita Castle?"

"Rita?" He shrugged elaborately. "Just another pony," he said. "Neat in her habits, minded her own business. I doubt we ever exchanged more than half a dozen words."

"She never . . . flirted with you? Just in fun."

"Not a bit," he said. "Maybe with other men, I wouldn't know about that, but never with me."

"How frequently would you say you saw her?"

"I suppose . . . once a month, maybe a little less. At parties, that's all. I never ran into her in town or anything."

"I see." I got to my feet. "Thank you for your time." I started for the elevator, and Kerrigan fell into step beside me.

Lydon trailed after us, saying in some confusion, "Is that it? Nothing else you want to know?"

"Maybe later on," I said casually, over my shoulder. We went out to the red-carpeted foyer and I pushed the button for the elevator.

"It's all so abrupt," said Lydon, standing nervously beside us, fidgeting from one foot to the other. His earlier sardonic manner had suddenly washed away without a trace. "You come in, you go out, I didn't even get to offer you a drink."

"Thanks just the same," I said.

The elevator came and we got aboard and pushed the

ground-floor button. The doors slid shut, cutting off my view of Lydon's bewildered and flustered face.

As we rode down, Kerrigan said, "I suppose he was lying about Rita."

"I should think so," I said.

"She made a pass at everybody in sight," he said. "There's no reason to skip Joe Lydon."

I said, "I suppose he's lying now because he took her up on it when she approached him."

"You think he's our man?"

"I have no idea. There's no reason to suppose she did anything but turn him down. Embarrassment and humiliation would make him tell the same lie now as if he were guilty of murder."

"He's still the best shot so far," Kerrigan insisted

"Possibly," I said. I saw no point in adding that he himself seemed a much more likely object for Rita Castle's illicit passion than did Joseph Lydon.

Besides, my main attention at the moment wasn't directly on Lydon or the problem of Rita Castle at all, but was on myself. I was noticing, with some sardonic amusement, how I was beginning to behave like the old fire horse who's heard the alarm bell. Despite myself my interest in this job was growing, and I was becoming impatient to see the rest of the actors, to hear their voices, read their faces and their houses, sniff of their private lives.

And that note; I wanted to see once more that note from Rita Castle.

15

There was one interview left tonight, with an airline executive named Paul Einhorn, and for that we headed back to Manhattan in yet another cab, bucketing westward along the Long Island Expressway.

During the trip, as usual, Kerrigan filled me in on the man we were to see. Einhorn, like Lydon, was a second-generation associate, a man whose father had been directly involved in the rackets, while the son's involvement was much more indirect. The significant differences between Einhorn and Lydon were that Einhorn was single, that Einhorn's mobster father and two mobster uncles were all still alive, and that Einhorn had made the break into legitimate business himself, rather than riding along with his father as Lydon had done.

"Paul is what you might call a slummer," Kerrigan said. "He's strictly in a square business, works for one of the big airlines companies, but through his father and his uncles he's got this in and he gets a kick out of being around real gangsters." A touch of sarcasm twisted the last few words of the sentence.

I said, "There's no mutual back-scratching? With Lydon there is."

"Not a bit of it," said Kerrigan. "Wait till you see him, you'll see why."

"Would I know about his father?"

"I don't know. Mike Einhorn, he used to operate in the

city here years ago, him and his two brothers."

"Where are they now?"

"Florida."

"Still in the corporation?"

Kerrigan grinned. "Still in."

"But the son isn't."

"Like I say, wait till you see him."

I said, "It seems as though the more people I see, the further I get away from the mob. Doesn't Rembek have any professional friends?"

Kerrigan shrugged and said, "Well, there's me. And Eustace Canfield. And that accountant you met, Pietrojetti. There were others on the list Ernie made up, too, but they've all got alibis."

"What a coincidence."

"Not so much," he said. "A man in the corporation, he has a natural tendency to keep himself covered, just in case. He lives his life as though tomorrow he'll have to explain it all in court."

"You mean the alibis might be faked?"

"No, I mean people who get harassment from the cops after a while learn to know where they were at such and such a time, and be able to prove it."

I almost made an angry automatic response, to deny police harassment of anyone, but stopped myself in time. In the first place, what Kerrigan said was true, there was harassment of known professional criminals because sometimes it paid off. And in the second place, what difference did it make what Kerrigan said or whether or not I defended the Department?

Paul Einhorn lived in Greenwich Village, an area of the city in which everything has changed in the last generation but the name. The artists and writers and bohemians who made that name famous are mostly gone now, and in their places are the young middle-class white-collar workers whose lives are enriched by a Greenwich Village address. Modern apartment buildings—exactly like those in, say, the Jamaica section of Queens—have been built on the old landmarks to house these people, and in one of them we found Paul Einhorn.

He was very drunk. He met us at the door with that foolish grin to be found on the faces of people who get drunk in order to have an excuse for their offensive behavior. "Couldn't wait," he announced. "Had to go on ahead. Come on in and catch up."

He staggered away from the door, leaving it open, slopping his drink on the parquet floor as he went. Kerrigan and I entered, shut the door, and followed him into an underfurnished modern living room with a view of Sheridan Square.

Einhorn was at a portable bar, his back to us. He was wearing black trousers, white shirt, black bow tie, white dinner jacket, but neither socks nor shoes. He was about twenty-five, with fine sandy hair already showing a tendency to thin. He was tall and very slender, with a good-looking but somewhat lax face, on which a little Errol Flynn mustache looked like an appeal for pity.

Over his shoulder, as he stood unsteadily at the bar, he called, "What's your pleasure, gents?"

I said to Kerrigan, "Put some steel in him."

Kerrigan grinned at me and nodded and went across the room to where Einhorn was clattering glasses and bottles together, weaving as he stood at the bar, his head sunk forward onto his chest. Kerrigan put an arm across Einhorn's shoulders and leaned his head close and began to murmur to Einhorn, who stopped moving his hands among the glasses and bottles and who appeared either to be listening intently or to have gone to sleep.

A stereo phonograph was playing slow jazz. I went over to the window and looked out at Sheridan Square, which is always surprisingly dark, much darker than an intersection that large and busy should be. Traffic thudded south on Seventh Avenue, a Volkswagen turned very slowly into Christopher Street, a cab picked up a young couple in front of Jack Delaney's restaurant. Out of the subway exit by the all-night newsstand came a young girl—under twenty, I mean—carrying something that looked like a violin case, only bigger. Maybe a cello case. She crossed Seventh Avenue when the light changed, lugging the cello case, and disappeared into Grove Street.

Kerrigan said, "Mister Tobin."

I turned and saw Einhorn over by the telephone, slowly dialing, giving the project all his concentration. Kerrigan, in the middle of the room, said to me, "Paul's calling down to the deli for coffee. Care for anything?"

His expression told me we were humoring Einhorn, so I said, "Thanks. A coffee regular would be good."

Einhorn had finished dialing by now. Kerrigan went over and helped him give the order. Whatever he'd said to the boy earlier must have been impressive; Einhorn looked very nearly sober, and wide-eyed with apprehension.

When the order was successfully given, Kerrigan said, "Paul, why don't you go wash your face while we wait? Make you feel a lot better."

"Good idea," said Einhorn unsteadily. "Very good idea." Nodding slowly and carefully and interminably, he moved at a careful pace from the room

Kerrigan came over to me and said, "He'll be all right. Better wait till the coffee comes before you try to talk to him."

"All right."

"I told him if he didn't straighten up, Ernie'd have to tell his father he wasn't co-operating, and then the old man would make him come live with him in Florida again."

"He has trouble with his father?"

"They're different breeds." Kerrigan grinned and said, "Personally, I've always figured he was the milkman's boy. Anyway, you see why the corporation doesn't do business with him."

"This is frequent?"

"If frequent means all the time, the answer's yes."

On the phonograph, the record came to a quiet end. We listened to the clicks of machinery, and then an album of jazz guitar began. I turned back to the view again and watched things happen on Sheridan Square, seeing the elderly delivery boy coming across the street in his apron with a green paper bag containing our order.

He arrived before Einhorn came back from washing up. Kerrigan paid, showed the delivery boy out, and said to me, "I'll get Paul."

"All right."

I stood by the window, watching the street and listening to the music, and I found myself playing the game called Might Have Been. It is a game played by people who are having trouble ignoring how intolerable their lives have become. Night scenes and guitar music are two powerful stimulants of the game.

What was I doing here, in this sad room, looking at that sad street, listening to that sad music, involving myself in all these sad lives? How came I here?

I was trying to open the window when Kerrigan came back into the room, running, crying, "He's gone!"

"I know," I said, still struggling with the window. "He just went out, he's down—"

There he was, shoes on now, trotting diagonally across the Square. Before I could get the damn window open he'd flagged a cab. In it, he disappeared down Seventh Avenue.

16

I said to Ernie Rembek, "I hope we're not disturbing your wife."

"She isn't here," he said impatiently. "She's away. Come on in, tell me about it."

We'd already told him about it, or at least Kerrigan had, over the phone from Einhorn's place. But Rembek had insisted we come directly over to his apartment to give him the complete story. Because there were things I wanted to see Rembek for myself, I'd agreed.

Now we were here, having been let in by the same formally dressed football player as the first time. This time, however, we hadn't been delivered to the office, but instead were ushered to a sort of den or library, a very masculine and even stuffy place that looked most like some organization's clubroom rather than like a room in a private home. Black leather chairs and sofas, dark wood built-in bookcases floor to ceiling, long dark draperies over the windows; all it lacked was two or three elderly members sleeping in the chairs.

Rembek was, with some impatience, insisting on playing host, and I agreed to a Scotch and water, which the football player went away to get, along with Kerrigan's Jack Daniels on the rocks. Rembek already had a brandy and a cigar going.

Now, all three of us sitting around like new members of the club, Rembek asked me again to tell him all about it.

"You already know all about it," I said. "We told you the

whole thing on the phone."

"Tell me again."

"He was drunk when we got there. Kerrigan used some slight pressure to get him to straighten up. He phoned a delicatessen for coffee, and then went off to wash his face. At Kerrigan's suggestion."

Rembek looked hard at Kerrigan. "Why?" he demanded.

I said, "It was the right thing to suggest. If Kerrigan hadn't done it, I would have. Einhorn needed cold water on his face, among other things. At any rate, the coffee was delivered, and then Kerrigan went to get Einhorn and he was gone. I was looking out the living-room window, and just as Kerrigan came back with the news I saw Einhorn leave the building and get into a cab."

"Which way did the cab go?"

"That doesn't matter. Seventh Avenue is one-way south, so the cab went south. He could have been heading anywhere."

Rembek chewed angrily on his cigar. After a minute he said, "Well? Do you think that's it?"

"Do I think that's what?"

"Damn it! Do you think he's the one? Did he kill Rita?"

"I don't know."

"Well, it looks like it, doesn't it? He ran, didn't he?"

"He was drunk," I said. "I understand he's afraid of his father."

Kerrigan said to Rembek, "I told the kid you'd have to tell Mike he wasn't co-operating if he didn't straighten up, and then Mike might make him go live down there again."

"Those morons," Rembek said in disgust.

I said, "Who? Einhorn and his father?"

"No. Mike Einhorn and his brothers. It's no wonder the son's the way he is."

110

"Why? Tell me about it."

But impatience was too strong in Rembek. Loudly he said, "What difference does it make? They're in Florida, for Christ's sake, *they* didn't kill Rita!"

"But maybe the son did," I said. "So tell me about his home in Florida. Why should he be so afraid to go back to it?"

Rembek took a deep breath, trying for a firm grip on the reins of his impatience, holding himself in check. "There are three Einhorn brothers," he said, "Mike and Sam and Alex. They live together and they think they're lumberjacks, all three of them. Indian wrestling, you know the sort? They've got a swimming pool on the grounds, they're constantly racing each other back and forth. Or they'll bring up a whore from Miami, they'll make bets which of them can put it to her the most times before six o'clock."

"Very hairy-chested," Kerrigan put in quietly. "Paul's more delicate."

"If there's any such thing as a heterosexual faggot," Rembek said, "Paul's it."

I said, "Where's his mother?"

Rembek shrugged. "Who knows? She was some bimbo Mike married when he was too drunk to know better. She ran out when Paul was a baby."

I said, "I've got his occupation listed as airline executive. What does that mean exactly?"

"It means he works for Transocean Airways. Public relations."

"Did the corporation get him the job?"

"No. I suppose he talked his way into it at some cocktail party. He's one of your college-educated lushes, they've always got good desk jobs someplace, public relations or advertising or research-and-development or something like that. You know the kind I mean."

"And his only connection with the corporation is through his father?"

"Right."

"You don't do any smuggling through him or anything like that."

"You saw him," Rembek said. "Would you trust him with anything important?"

"No," I said.

Rembek shrugged. "Neither would we. He never made the offer and we never made the suggestion."

Kerrigan said, "He made an offer to me one time."

We both looked at him. Rembek said, "When was this?"

"Year or two ago, right after he got the job with the airline. He came up to me at a party and said, 'Anything you want from the old country, buddy, you want me to slip anything through customs, just give me the word.' He was stewed, so I said thanks, I'd let him know, and that's all either of us ever said about it."

Rembek said, "He never talked like that to me at all."

I said, "His father and uncles, are they retired?"

"Who, them? Not on your life. They run some gambling operations down there. Florida's a big state for bettors, you know."

"But they don't come up here at all?"

"Maybe once a year, not even that much."

"They wouldn't know Rita Castle."

Rembek snorted. "*Them?* I wouldn't introduce those crazy bastards to my cleaning woman."

"All right. You'll send some people to look for the son?"

"They're already out," Rembek said grimly.

"Frankly," I said, "I doubt he's our man. So he should be treated gently."

"Don't worry," he said. "The boys I sent out aren't supposed to do anything but find him."

"Good."

Rembek sipped at his brandy, put it aside, and said, "You get anything else done tonight?"

"I saw some people," I said. "I don't have anything to report yet."

"I'll have alibi reports on the six new ones by tomorrow morning," he said. "You want them sent to the office?"

"Yes. There'll be someone there after nine o'clock."

"Right. I also spread the word around a little, about what you're doing. If anybody knows anything or finds out anything, they're supposed to get in touch with you at the office."

"Good." I set my drink down and said, "There were a couple of matters I wanted to go over with you tomorrow, but as long as I'm here I might as well take care of them now."

"Go ahead," he said.

"I told you about being contacted by two Homicide detectives. One of them suggested you might have hired me to help smoke-screen the fact that you killed Rita Castle yourself. I said I didn't believe it, and I still don't believe it. But it is possible. She ran out, you found her, you killed her and took back the money. Then you hired me to stir things up, muddy the waters a little."

Rembek gave a crooked grin and said, "Does that sound like my style?"

"No," I admitted. "But I'd like to cover every possibility."

"Meaning what?"

"Meaning I'd like your alibi for Wednesday night, too. Could I have it with the others tomorrow morning?"

"I can give it to you right now," he said.

"I mean, verified," I said.

He shook his head. "You aren't going to get it verified. I spent Wednesday night here, all by myself. I can't even have

Eleanor—have my wife verify it. She wasn't here."

"Where was she?"

"Visiting friends," he said shortly.

"The same place she is now?"

"She's spending a couple of weeks," he said.

"When did she leave?"

"Why? What difference does it make?"

"I don't know, maybe none. When did she leave?"

"Sunday. I had to go to Baltimore over Sunday night to a meeting, so when I left she went up to—she left the same time I did. Let's get off this, it doesn't have any connection."

"Your wife didn't know Rita Castle?"

"Of course not."

"Are you sure?"

"Positive. I told you before how I feel about my wife. I wouldn't hurt her with a thing like that."

"Her brother wouldn't tell her?"

"Frank Donner? Definitely not. He knows how things are."

"All right. The other thing is George Lewis, your friend on the Coast."

"What about him?"

"He knew Rita. Let's make sure he was actually out on the Coast on Wednesday night."

"Can do. Anything else?"

"Not now."

We finished our drinks and Rembek rang for the football player to show us out, he himself staying behind in his club-room.

At the entrance foyer, I stopped to say to the football player, "What time did Mister Rembek get back Wednesday night?"

He looked surprised, then turned silently to Kerrigan, obviously wanting clearance from him before answering me. Kerrigan frowned at me, hesitating, and then nodded briefly. The football player said, "About four o'clock sir."

"Thanks."

Kerrigan said to him, "There's no point worrying Ernie about having told us that. Got it?"

"Yes, sir."

We left the apartment and rang for the elevator. Kerrigan didn't speak again until we were in the elevator and on our way down. Then he said, "What made you ask him that?"

"I had the feeling Rembek was lying."

"Why?"

"He was too cheerful about not having verification. If the story was straight he would have said he didn't have any verification but his bodyguard."

Kerrigan said, carefully, "Let me get this straight. You think he *did* do it? Like your cop friend said?"

"No. I think he had another reason for lying. You can come with me and help me try to prove it."

"Sure."

We walked the two blocks to Rita Castle's apartment building. When we'd first gone there I'd seen that the doorman recognized Kerrigan and seemed to understand the essence of his relationship with Rembek so now I told Kerrigan to explain to the doorman it was okay to answer my questions. He said, "I don't get it, but all right."

We talked briefly with the doorman, Kerrigan first giving him a capsule explanation, sufficient to get him to talk without actually telling him anything. Then I said, "The early part of the week, Mister Rembek spent a lot of time here by himself, didn't he?"

"Yes, sir," he said. He kept blinking the whole time we talked, more than half convinced he was going to get into trouble in this situation no matter which way he went.

I said, "Did he come here Wednesday night?"

"Yes, sir."

"What time did he get here?"

"About eleven o'clock."

"And what time did he leave?"

"I guess around four."

"You guess?"

"Around four. Maybe five of."

"Thanks," I said.

We went back out on the sidewalk and Kerrigan said, "I don't get it."

"Ernie Rembek is a more emotional man than he wants anybody to know. After Rita left him, he kept going back to her apartment, just sitting there, thinking about her."

"You mean, waiting for her to come back?"

"Not really. Just thinking about her, remembering her. Walking around the apartment, being very emotional all by himself. Now he's embarrassed about it and ashamed of it and he doesn't want anybody to know about it."

"I never would have thought it of Ernie," Kerrigan said.

"That's why," I said, and a limousine stopped at the curb and Ernie Rembek hopped out.

He came angrily over the sidewalk to me, saying, "I thought I'd catch up with you here. What's the idea pumping my man?"

"You were obscuring the issue with a useless lie," I said. "I had to clear it out of the way before I could go any further."

"You're wasting time," he started; and I interrupted him, saying, "No, *you're* wasting time. My time. If you want me to do my best, tell me the truth when I ask you a question."

He started to say something, then changed his mind. He turned to Kerrigan and said, "Goodnight, Roger."

Kerrigan seemed surprised, but he recovered well. "Right. See you, Ernie." He said to me, "What time do we start tomorrow?"

"I don't know yet. Call me at the office around ten."

"Will do."

He went away down the street. When he was out of earshot, Rembek said to me, "All right, you're right. I didn't think it made any difference where I was, I knew I didn't do anything to Rita."

"But I have to know it."

"Okay. Are you satisfied now?"

"Yes." I saw the doorman looking out the glass doors at us, a worried expression on his face. I said, "Why not go tell him everything's okay? He's pretty upset."

"Right. Then can I give you a lift?"

"To the subway."

"Will do."

We did no more talking about his whereabouts Wednesday night.

17

The sound of rain woke me before seven on Saturday morning. I hurried into my clothes and went out back to cover the hole with tarpaulins. From now on I would have to put the first layer or two of concrete block down as I went along, so rain wouldn't have a chance to cause cave-ins or alter the dimensions of the hole. Maybe, if the rain let up later on, I could put the blocks down in the first part this afternoon.

I didn't think of the job until later on, when I was sitting in the kitchen drinking my first cup of coffee and watching Kate, in her robe, moving back and forth as she readied breakfast. Then it occurred to me that Kate wouldn't be going to work today because I had become the breadwinner around here again.

The thought didn't cheer me. In the course of moving around Ernie Rembek's world yesterday I had gradually built up a professional enthusiasm for the task at hand, but the enthusiasm hadn't survived until this morning. I wanted to fill my attention with the wall, with the problems caused by rain, and instead I was being dragged away into this other thing, this mean and petty shuffling through degraded lives in a pointless quest for the slayer of a whore. What did I care about Rita Castle? What did I care about anything?

I even toyed with the notion of sending Ernie Rembek back his five thousand dollars—I could telegraph it to him, I wouldn't even have to go to Manhattan—but the presence of

Kate, here in the kitchen with me, made it impossible. Both because my quitting would mean she would have to go to work herself today after all, and because she was putting so much hope into the beneficial results she was hoping this Rembek job would bring.

So I tried to turn my attention to the job, and with some difficulty I did manage to do some thinking about it, to recall to mind the five suspects I had seen last night. Were any of them at all likely?

Einhorn first. He had run away, but I took that to be more a sign of character than of guilt. He was a young man who would run away from anything, which would most likely include overtures from Rita Castle. He was unlikely.

Hogan, the one who admitted to having "inspected" Rita when she annoyed him. His character too seemed wrong for the man I was after, too self-contained, too machined, too brisk and neat. I visualized the killer as a sloppier man, a man whose emotional and/or financial sloppiness had finally resolved themselves in the ultimate sloppiness of murder.

Lydon, the real-estate man with the view. He seemed sloppy enough, but was unlikely from the other direction. I could imagine Rita Castle going off with either Einhorn or Hogan—the first because she could dominate him and the second because he could dominate her—but I couldn't see at all where she would have gone off with Lydon. Besides, if money were the killer's object—and it did seem to have been so—Lydon's position was surely such that he could get all the money he might need in less violent and dangerous ways.

Donner, family man, Rembek's brother-in-law. I had trouble thinking about him. His marriage seemed too good to be true, but wasn't that merely special pleading, my own personal requirements coloring my perspective? Until I found

119

definite evidence about Frank Donner one way or the other, I would merely keep his name on the list, active but not very.

Kerrigan. So far, I thought him the likeliest. He had the youth and style to attract a Rita Castle, he gave indications of having the ruthlessness necessary to work out this sort of plot for money, and he apparently had no current liaison with a woman, a point I would have to check on. Phase two, then, should probably concentrate on Kerrigan.

By quarter after nine I'd thought myself back into the case again, however lukewarmly, and I went to the phone to call the office and tell Mickey Hansel I'd be in shortly after ten, and to give him a message to pass on to Kerrigan: Please come into the office at eleven.

But the phone rang three times without an answer, and then was abruptly replaced by the voice of an operator, asking me what number I was calling. I told her, and she said that number was temporarily disconnected, out of order, she couldn't say exactly how long it would be until service was resumed. I thanked her and hung up and the phone immediately rang.

It was Ernie Rembek. "Trouble," he said.

"What kind of trouble?"

"Your office just blew up."

"What?"

"I just got a call from the building. It happened ten minutes ago. Hansel was in there. Did you have some kind of dynamite around or something?"

"Of course not. How is Hansel?"

"How would he be? He's dead."

I said, "Our man thinks I'm closer to him than I am."

"You aren't holding out on me?"

"No."

"Can you come in here right away?"

120

"Not until I get my family moved somewhere safe."

"All right. Naturally."

"Can you outfit me with a gun?"

"No problem."

"Hip holster, that's what I'm used to."

"You'll get regular police issue," he promised.

"Good."

"We might have trouble getting you a permit, that's the only thing."

"I'll carry it without, if I have to."

"That's the way," he said. "How long before you get here?"

"I don't know. I'll be there as soon as I can."

Fortunately it was Saturday and Bill wasn't in school. I went upstairs to where Kate was making the beds and told her what had happened and that it would be best if she and Bill moved out of the house for a while. She said, "Mitch, should you get out of the whole thing?"

"It's too late, he's already after me. Start packing, I'll call Bill in."

"Where should we go?"

"How about Grace?" I said, meaning her sister out on Long Island, in Patchogue.

"I'll call her," she said.

Bill was in a garage across the street, working with a neighbor boy on a broken bicycle chain. I called him in and told him he and his mother would be going to visit Uncle Alfred and Aunt Grace for a while. He made the sour face appropriate to the occasion and said, "How come?"

I said, "Because the job I'm on is getting dangerous. I want you to keep an eye out and protect your mother."

A little more pep talk along the same line got him into the proper mood, and he went upstairs to pack just as the phone started ringing again.

This time it was Marty Kengelberg, my old friend from Homicide. He said, "Good, I got you at home. Stick around there, will you, Mitch?"

"What for?"

"Fred and I want to have a talk with you."

"Could you make it soon? I'm having kind of a busy day."

"So are we, Mitch. We'll get there as soon as we can."

I hung up and helped Kate and Bill carry their luggage out to the car. Kate stood with me in the front hallway a minute. We'd never been very much on expressing our feelings to one another, and in the rare moments like this one it was a handicap. But Kate said it all by simply reaching up and touching her fingertips to the side of my face.

"Nothing will happen," I promised her. I kissed her and she went out to the car in the rain and drove away.

I called Rembek back and told him two detectives from Homicide were coming to see me, so I'd be later than I thought. Then I said, "Could they be coming because of this explosion?"

"How do I know?"

"Under what name was that office set up?"

"Not yours."

"All right. I'll get into town as soon as I can."

Then there was nothing to do but wait. When at last the doorbell rang, I looked at my watch and it was ten minutes past eleven.

Marty had the same partner with him this time, the disbeliever named Fred James. They shrugged out of their raincoats, I invited them into the living room, and Marty said, "Have you heard about the explosion?"

So that was that. I said, "Yes. How do you know about the connection?"

"What difference does it make?"

"One, you were following me. Two, you were tipped."

Marty shrugged. "We were following you."

"So you have a lot to talk to me about."

"Beginning with the explosion."

"Right." I recrossed my legs the other way and said, "Ernie Rembek just called and told me. He said the explosion happened, he said a guy named Mickey Hansel was killed in it. That's all he said."

"Do you know this Mickey Hansel?"

"Yes. Rembek gave him to me yesterday to be my file clerk. He had a key and was supposed to get to the office at nine this morning, do some filing I left for him, and take messages."

Fred James said, "He was five minutes late."

"Then he had an five extra minutes to live, didn't he?"

Marty said, "What kind of explosive did you have in there?"

"Come on, Marty."

"You mean you didn't have any?"

"No. I didn't have any."

"So what do you think it was, a booby trap?"

"I suppose so."

"Aimed at you."

"Seems that way."

Marty abruptly looked around and said, "Where's Kate?"

"Gone to visit her sister a few days."

They looked at each other, and Fred James said to me, "Looks as though you found something out."

"It looks that way," I agreed. "But if I did, I don't know what it is."

Marty frowned at me. "You don't have a lead?"

"Not a one. I've got a long list of suspects, that's all."

"You went to see four people last night," he said, "not counting Rembek. We want their names and what they told you."

I shook my head. "No, Marty. That isn't the deal."

"It is now. There's been a second murder, and this one's in our jurisdiction."

"The answer is no."

Fred James said, using my first name without the right to do so, "Come on, Mitch, be sensible. You've been a cop, you know what we can do if you give us a bad time. You want to spend the next three weeks in the Tombs as a material witness?"

"Three hours, you mean," I said. "People with access to Ernie Rembek's lawyers never spend three weeks in the Tombs."

Marty said, "We aren't trying to threaten you, Mitch."

"Maybe you aren't. Your partner was."

Fred James said, "It looks like I just rub you the wrong way, Mitch. I'm sorry about that."

"So am I," I said.

Marty said, "Why do you want to hold out on us, Mitch?"

"I don't want to spoil my effectiveness. If you keep showing up where I've just been, knowing everything that was said to me, Rembek is going to tell his people to stop answering me."

Marty knew that was true, and his knowledge showed in his face. Nevertheless he said, "It just doesn't feel right, Mitch, you holding out. You know we'd be careful how we used what you told us."

"I don't know that at all. I still know how the cop's mind works, Marty, and I know a promise to somebody on the other side of the fence is just tactics."

"Are you on the other side of the fence?"

124

"I'm working for Ernie Rembek right now."

"Frankly, Mitch," Fred James said, "that's what sticks in my craw. You know? It sticks in my craw."

"Maybe you'll choke on it, Fred," I said.

Marty said, hurriedly, "Okay, Mitch, don't get your back up. Fred doesn't know you as good as I do, that's all."

"You think you know me, Marty? Come along and listen."

They followed me out to the hall, where I picked up the phone and called Ernie Rembek again. When he came on the line I said, "Those two detectives I told you about are here. They tell me they had me followed all day yesterday. They know the addresses I went to last night, but they don't know for sure yet who I visited in each place."

Rembek said, "They're asking you?"

"Yes."

"And?"

"I'm not telling."

"Good," he said.

"The only problem is," I said, "if they're following me around I can't do the job right. They won't have that much trouble finding the right tenant in each of those buildings, and then they'll go in asking questions and making trouble. You don't want that happening everywhere I go."

Rembek said, "You're goddamn right I don't."

"So I've got to quit," I said. "I'm sorry, but I'm hamstrung. If you want me to send the money back, I'll—"

I was interrupted simultaneously by Rembek and Marty, Rembek shouting, "What the hell—" and Marty saying urgently, "Wait a minute! Mitch, listen! Wait a minute!"

"Hold on a second," I said into the phone, cupped my hand over the mouthpiece, and said to Marty, "What is it?"

"We don't want you to *quit*, for God's sake!"

"I don't have any choice." I could hear Rembek still yammering away, but I ignored him.

Marty said, "We'll lay off, Mitch. Guaranteed."

"What kind of a guarantee?"

Fred James said, sarcastically, "You want it in writing, Mitch?"

Marty surprised him by turning on him and snapping, "Shut up, Fred! This man isn't kidding, he'll do what he says."

"I'll always do what I say."

Marty turned back to me. "So will I. And I guarantee you won't be followed any more, and the people you saw last night won't be questioned. When you've got something you want to tell me, you just get in touch, that's all. Otherwise, we'll leave you strictly alone."

"That's a promise you can't make, Marty, and we both know it."

"Let me make a call," he said.

Rembek was still yammering. I said into the phone, "I'll call you back," broke the connection, and gave the phone to Marty.

It took him two calls to do it, one to his headquarters and one to Centre Street, with complicated explanations both times, but when he was done I was a free agent again. He hung up from the second call and said to me, "There. You satisfied?"

"Completely."

"I'll see you, Mitch," he said.

"I'll be in touch, Marty."

Fred James and I didn't exchange farewells.

After they left I called Rembek back again. He came on the line and said, "Did it work?"

"Yes."

He chuckled. "You had me going for a minute there. I thought you meant it."

"If it hadn't worked," I told him, "I meant it."

18

The doorman recognized me now. I'd taken a cab from the subway, because of the rain, and he came and opened the door and touched his cap brim and called me sir, treating me with the same deferential respect he gave notaries like Wickler, the messenger who had brought me the first news of this job. Getting out of the cab and standing under a canopy that protected me from the rain, following the deferential door man into the building, I remembered Ernie Rembek in our first meeting, assuring me that no one wanted my cherry, and I wondered if I wasn't perhaps somehow losing it anyway, through no fault of anyone.

I must find the murderer very quickly, and get out of this world. With my wall lay safety.

Upstairs, Rembek himself opened the door for me. He told me my new office was to be right here, in his apartment, and he escorted me to it, saying, "Nobody's going to mine *this* place, I guarantee it."

He led me to a small room with a view of an air shaft. There was the same sort of furniture as in the first office, desk and filing cabinet and chair and typewriter stand. Rembek stood in the doorway with me, looking at it, and said, "How is it?"

"It's fine."

"There's your gun in the bottom desk drawer. I'm sorry, I couldn't get a permit for you."

"That's all right."

127

I went over and opened the drawer and took out the gun, a Colt Cobra, a snub-nosed revolver chambered for the .38 Special. It was about the same size and weight as the gun I'd worn for the last several years on the force, a Smith & Wesson Chief's Special which had also fired the .38 Special, the only difference being that this Colt had a hammer shroud and my old S&W hadn't.

There was a good plain hip holster in the drawer, too. I threaded it into my belt, tucked the nose of the holster into my hip pocket, and slid the revolver into place.

Memories flooded back like the sudden blare of a radio.

Rembek said, "Well, how is it? Okay?"

"Go away for a while," I said. "Come back in five minutes."

He didn't understand me. "What? What's the matter with you?"

I turned on him, talking loudly in order to be able to talk at all, shouting, "Damn it, Rembek get out of here! Go *away* for five minutes!"

I don't know if he understood then or not, but at least he went away, shutting the door behind him, leaving me alone in the little square room with the weight of the gun on my right hip.

How could I have forgotten about that? For eighteen years I had worn a gun, most of the time right there, on my hip, the weight known and familiar and comforting. The first month or two after . . . afterward, I walked oddly, feeling wrong and misshapen because that weight wasn't there, almost as though a hole had been bitten into my hip.

But the body forgets, too, as does the mind, and as time had gone on I had grown used to that emptiness on my hip, and had stopped noticing that anything was missing there, and so I was unprepared when I put this new gun on, my guard was down and the memories came in with long brass nails and clawed the inside of my chest.

Everything passes. Soon it was possible for me to breathe again, and to move, and to distract my attention with thoughts of other things. When, five minutes later, the knock sounded at the door, I was sitting at the desk looking at the alibi reports on the six from Rembek's second list, which had been in a manila envelope atop the desk, waiting for me.

I called, "Come in," and Rembek entered, looking hesitant. "It's all right," I told him. "Come on in."

He came the rest of the way in, leaving the door open. "Sometimes you confuse me, Mister Tobin," he said.

"If I were an entirely rational and comprehensible man," I told him, "I would still be on the force, and someone else would be working for you." I motioned at the alibi reports. "I see we've eliminated four of those."

"Three," he said.

"We can cross Mickey Hansel off now," I said.

"Oh, yeah. I'm sorry, I didn't make the connection."

I looked again at the alibi reports. One of the two remaining suspects from this list was William Pietrojetti, the accountant I'd met my first time up here, who claimed to have spent the evening at home alone, and the other was a man named Matthew Seay, occupation bodyguard, who stated he'd been with a friend all night Wednesday but who would give no further details.

I said, "This Seay, is he the one who opens your door here?"

"No, that's Burger, he stays here all the time. He never met Rita at all. Seay's gone with me sometimes to social affairs and stuff like that."

"I want to see him. And Pietrojetti, too. In their homes, like the others."

"This afternoon good?"

129

"The sooner the better."

He nodded. "Done."

I said, "What about George Lewis? Was he on the Coast Wednesday night?"

"Definitely."

"Good." I got out pencil and paper, started to make up a list.

Rembek said, "I've got you a new gopher. He'll be here in less than an hour."

"No, that's all right, I don't need one any more."

He looked at me. "You feel bad about Hansel, huh?"

"Naturally. Will I get copies of the police reports on the explosion?"

"As soon as there are any."

"Good."

I finished my list, the seven active names:

> Roger Kerrigan
> Frank Donner
> Louis Hogan
> Joseph Lydon
> Paul Einhorn
> William Pietrojetti
> Matthew Seay

I gave the list to Rembek, saying, "I'd like a complete rundown on the police records, if any, of these seven."

He took the list almost greedily, studying the names. "It's down to these, is that it? It's one of these seven."

"Maybe. If we read that note right." I shook my head. "I'm sorry to lose that note."

"You left it in the office?"

"Yes."

"If you want to know what it said," he said bitterly, "just

ask me. I know it by heart."

"That's good." I went over and sat down and pulled the typewriter close. "Reel it off."

He did, in a monotone, and if it gave him pain he made no sign of it. " 'I am going away. I have found a real man and we are going to find a new life together far away. You'll never see either of us again.' "

"Okay, fine." I took the sheet out of the typewriter and laid it face down on the desk. "Look at that list I just gave you," I said. "Which of those seven would have known about the cash Rita took?"

He studied the list, frowning. "Well, Roger would. And Frank? Frank Donner. Pietrojetti would, naturally. Matt Seay might, he's my bodyguard sometimes, he might have been along once or twice when I unloaded some of it. Lou Hogan wouldn't. Neither would Joe Lydon, Paul Einhorn, neither of them." He looked at me. "But *she* knew about it, she could have told the guy herself."

"Then he wouldn't have been after the money from the beginning," I said. "She wouldn't have told him about the money before they were . . . close. So if he was after it from the beginning, he had to know it from somebody other than her."

"So these three are out? Lou, and Joe, and Paul?"

"No. They're just more unlikely than the others. It could still be one of them, and the affair started out of passion, and the money didn't come into it until later."

He looked at the list some more. "For one reason or other, you could cross off every name on this list."

"That's why I'm not crossing any of them off yet. Tell me about the building."

"What building?"

"Where my office was yesterday. Does the corporation

just have that one office there, or the whole building, or what?"

"We've got maybe half a dozen offices in there, for this and that. The rest of the building is square."

"The corporation owns it?"

"As a matter of fact, Joe Lydon owns it. I told you, we lease a lot of property from him here and there."

"So he'd have a key to let him into the building."

"He wouldn't need a key. It's a twenty-four-hour building, there's an old guy on duty at the door and elevator all night long. And he wouldn't need a key for the office door either, that kind of lock you can go through with a toothpick."

I said, "So that doesn't cut it down any." I looked around at my new empty desk and said, "There's some paperwork I'm going to have to replace. You've got another copy of the alibi reports from your first list, haven't you?"

"Right. In my office. I'll bring them in to you."

"Good. And the police reports from Allentown, I'll need to replace those."

"Is that a definite must? It'll be tough to get another set by now."

"We'll have to try," I said.

He shrugged. "If you say so."

I took out my notebook and opened to the section where I'd copied the names from the address book in Rita Castle's apartment. I said, "What was the name of Rita's boy friend when you met her, do you remember?"

"What the hell do you want with *him?* She hasn't seen him in two years."

"I want to talk to him. What was his name?"

"Quigley. Something Quigley, I forget the first name."

I flipped through the notebook. "Ted," I said. "Ted Quigley."

He frowned at me and at the notebook. "Where'd you get that?"

"Maybe she didn't see him," I said, "but she kept his name and address and phone number in her address book."

"She did?" He half shook his head, then shrugged it off, saying, "It was a fossil, it was left over, an old address book."

"Probably," I said. I got to my feet. "I'll be back after a while."

"Why? Where are you going?"

"To talk to Ted Quigley."

"What's the point?"

"I'll tell you when I come back." I stopped and looked at him and said, "Don't get excited about it, Rembek. I don't think Ted Quigley came out of the past and took Rita away."

"Then what do you want to see him for?"

"I want to find out who he thinks she was. I feel a little confusion about her sometimes."

He started to say something, fast and angry, and then abruptly stopped. "Yes," he said, in a different tone. "So do I. Maybe I had her wrong all along. I did, I had her wrong all along."

"I'll be back soon," I said, and started out the door.

He said, "Hold on, I'll get Roger."

"I don't need Kerrigan this trip."

"But—"

"He observes me when I talk to people in the corporation. Ted Quigley isn't in the corporation." That reminded me of something. I stopped and said, "Just for the record, where *did* you meet Rita Castle?"

"At a backers' audition. She was reading one of the parts."

"There's no links there that I don't know about?"

"No. I didn't invest in the production, and she didn't play in it when it was performed. I heard it died in New Haven."

"All right. I'll be back soon."

As I was going out the door he called after me, "Mister Tobin?"

I turned and looked at him.

He said, "Tell me what Quigley says, will you? Who he thinks she was."

19

Ted Quigley lived on East 10th Street, way over between Avenue A and Avenue B, facing the blacktopped and link-fenced playground called Tompkins Square. It is deeply within the section known as the Lower East Side, a slum area of low rents and crowded apartment buildings. The area around East 10th and Avenue B has come to be the closest thing to an artists' colony in Manhattan today, as the high rents paid in Greenwich Village by the white-collar workers have forced the artists and bohemians out.

Quigley lived in a third-floor walk-up in a narrow old building with a coffee house on the first floor. I knocked on his door and got no answer, tried the knob and the door was locked. On the off-chance, I went downstairs to the coffee house, which was nearly empty at this time of day—just a little after one P.M.—and asked the woman washing cups in the sink at the back if she'd seen Ted Quigley around today.

She looked at me and I could see her smelling the odor of cop on me, an aura that doesn't strip away as easily as does the badge. I smiled and said, "No, I'm not a cop. On the level."

She wasn't sure whether to believe me or not, but my candor was in my favor. She hesitated, looking me over, and then shrugged and said, "Okay. If he isn't upstairs, he's probably at his girl's place. You know where that is?"

I shook my head. "No. And I don't know her name either.

I've never met Ted Quigley."

She was both curious and apprehensive. It wasn't that Ted Quigley was a criminal—my assumption was that he was not—it was just that I was on the short end of a pair of prejudices, smelling as I did of cop. People in poor neighborhoods are prejudiced against the police because they believe—sometimes with reason—that the police are prejudiced against them. Artists and bohemians, although not usually breakers of society's laws, are incessantly breakers of society's customs, which involves them with the police almost as much as the lawbreakers, with total lack of sympathy and comprehension on both sides. Being in a neighborhood of poor bohemians, I was feeling the brunt of these prejudices combined.

Still, I had given every indication of open honesty, and I was alone—policemen rarely enter such neighborhoods as this alone—and it seemed to her worth taking the chance on me. She said, "I'll give you the phone number, you can call and see if he's there."

"Thank you."

She had to look it up. I followed her to the cash register, where she got a dog-eared phone book and made a point of looking in it in such a way that I couldn't see the page. She wrote the number down on the back of an envelope with a stub of pencil, and then had an idea for further security, saying, "I'll dial it for you."

The pay phone was on the wall nearby, not in a booth. I gave her a dime and she dialed the number, then handed me the phone. She retired to the cash register, where she could hear my half of the conversation without making a point of it, and I listened to seven rings before the phone was answered by a girl whose voice sounded as though she were too young to be out of school. I said, "I was told Ted Quigley might be there."

"Hold on," she said, sounding very bored and world-weary, as though matters of moment in which she was engaged were constantly being interrupted by calls for Ted Quigley. Away from the phone I heard her holler, "It's for you!"

His voice sounded older, and yet with something very youthful in it, a sort of querulousness. He said, "Hello? What is it?"

"Ted, did you hear about Rita Castle?"

"Naturally," he said, as though I'd reminded him of an unanswered insult. "The *cops* told me."

"They've been around."

"You *bet* they've been around."

"Now I'm around," I said.

His voice immediately got more guarded. "What are you? More cops?"

"No. I'm on a kind of assignment. I'm supposed to find out who Rita Castle was."

"What for?" he demanded sarcastically. "*Screen Secrets?*"

"No. For Ernie Rembek. You know who he is?"

Silence.

"Ted?"

"Yeah." Very small voice. "I know who he is."

"He didn't kill her, Ted." Out of the corner of my eye I could see the woman at the cash register react to the word "kill" and then very quickly recover.

Meanwhile Ted Quigley said, in a loud voice, "Well, I didn't either!"

"Of course not, I know that."

"I've got an *alibi*. Even the *cops* had to take it."

"Ted, I never thought for a minute you killed her. All I ask from you is conversation. I want to know who Rita was."

"Why?"

"Because Ernie Rembek hired me to find out."

"Why does *he* want to know?"

"Ask him."

"Huh. Sure, any second now."

"I'm in the coffee house," I said. "Downstairs from your apartment. Could you come over? I'll buy you a cup of coffee, we'll talk for a few minutes."

"I'm not sure."

"There's no trouble for you in this, Ted, I guarantee it."

"You're in the coffee house?" he asked, and I knew what he was thinking. That I was already here, that all I had to do was hang around until he came home.

"I'm right here," I said.

"All right," he said. "Twenty minutes."

"Thanks, Ted."

I hung up and thanked the woman and ordered a cup of coffee. I sat at the table way at the back and drank my coffee and waited.

It took him only fifteen minutes, and he brought the girl with him. She looked older than she'd sounded on the phone, but my guess was that the voice was more accurate than the face.

I introduced myself by name—Mitch Tobin, the informal way—and Quigley introduced the girl as Robin. I said, "Ted, for just a few minutes I want to talk to you by yourself. Would Robin mind waiting for us, having a cup of coffee at another table?"

She answered for herself, saying, "Fine by me, pal," in an impudent manner, and swivel-hipped away to a table far down the long room. Both she and Quigley were dressed in loafers and dungarees and bulky sweaters. His hair was long and hers was much longer. He had a scraggly beard with blotches of skin showing through, as though he'd just recently gotten over a lingering sickness. Beards have a strange reverse effect these days; at first glance they make their wearer look older than he is, but at second glance the wearer looks like someone much younger than he is who is trying to look much older. As a result Ted Quigley, who was probably twenty-five or -six, looked like an eighteen-year-old wearing a beard in order to look thirty.

We three were the only customers in the long narrow room at the moment, and I could see the woman in charge being unhappy that what was obviously one group of people had split into two camps at opposite ends of the room. She came over reluctantly at my signal, and was not cheered by my order of three cups of coffee.

Quigley said, "Robin likes tea. Ceylon Breakfast. I'll take espresso."

The woman nodded and said to me, "Another cup of American?"

"Yes, thank you."

She went away, and Quigley said to me, "I've been thinking about this on the way over, and I think you're up to something. You've got some kind of racket, that's what I think. And the only reason I'm here is, I'm curious what your racket is."

I said, "Ernie Rembek is upset at what happened to Rita. I'm an ex-cop, he hired me to help find out who killed her."

"What are you, some kind of Sam Spade?"

"You mean, a private detective? No. I have no license, no official position at all. I'm working for Rembek as a private citizen."

"But you're out to get the killer," he said, being sardonic. "You're doing the Humphrey Bogart bit."

"If you say so."

He shook his head. "You're wrong for it," he said. "You're

overweight. The face is all wrong. You look more like a football coach."

I smiled, in spite of myself. "Not that bad, I hope."

"You're more the Barton MacLane type," he said.

I said, "It's too bad those movies weren't that good the
first time around. My friends and I didn't memorize any of
them. You used to go with Rita Castle, didn't you?"

Stung, he said, "What do you mean, *go* with her?"

I nodded toward Robin, at the front table. "You're going
with her now, aren't you?"

"I'm sleeping with her, if that's what you mean."

I looked at him in real amazement. "Are you trying to
shock me? Really?"

He shrugged, beginning to be uncomfortable. "It's up to
you," he said.

"If you think premarital sex is shocking," I said, "why
don't you stop it? It's bad enough to be a prude, you don't
have to be a hypocrite, too."

"All right," he said, "all right, that's enough of that. Never
mind my sex life."

"You used to sleep with Rita Castle, didn't you? That's
the way you want me to say it, right?"

He spread his hands. "All right," he said. "You can lay
off."

"You're done? No more movies, no more shockers?"

"I'm done," he said. He managed an uncertain smile. "I
just got up," he said, "I'm not with it yet. Yeah, I used to
sleep with Rita."

"That was two years ago?"

"More like two weeks ago," he said.

"What was that?"

"She used to come down to see me every once in a while,"
he said. He glanced over his shoulder, then leaned close

140

across the table and said, "Robin doesn't know about it."

"It looks like nobody knew about it."

"You mean Rembek? You *bet* he didn't know about it." Quigley gave a smug grin and said, "*He* thought he was gonna marry her."

"Marry? Are you sure?"

"That's what she told me. She said after she and Rembek got married we'd be able to spend more time together because men don't watch their wives as close as they watch their mistresses."

"Rembek already has a wife."

He waved a hand negligently. "I suppose he was gonna divorce her. Rita never said."

"And Rita was going to go through with the marriage?"

"She said so."

"What does that mean?"

He thought about his answer for a while, drumming his fingernails on the table top. Finally he said, "It was the gilded-cage bit. Rembek was rich and important, he could do a lot for her. It was great when he was just paying the rent, and she could still come down sometimes and see her old friends, and she had lots of cash and good clothes and the whole bit. But then Rembek decided he was in love with her and he wanted to marry her, and she didn't want to give up all the good stuff, so she said yes. But I don't know that she would have gone through with it."

"You think she might have run out?"

"Isn't that what she did?"

"How much do you know about what happened to her?"

"What I read in the paper."

"Yes, but what was that?"

He shrugged, indicating that he didn't see the point of the question but was willing to answer it. "It said she was killed in

141

a motel in Pennsylvania. I don't remember where."

"Is that all?"

"What else? It didn't say who did it, but it didn't have to."

"You mean you know?"

"It looks to me like she took off, and Rembek went after her and killed her. Isn't that how it looks to you?"

"I'm not sure. Why are you telling me this?"

"Why not?"

"I told you I'm working for Rembek."

"So what? I'm no threat to Mister Ernest Rembek, so it doesn't matter what I think. What am I going to do, go to the cops?"

"Maybe."

"With what? What proof? Besides, I'm me and he's him. What's my chances of getting the cops to pick him up on my say-so?"

"None," I said. "But up to now he doesn't know about Rita's continuing to see you. At least, I don't think he does."

"He's already killed her. It's a dead issue, excuse the pun. He wouldn't waste his time on me now. The only thing I can't figure out is why he'd hire anybody to find the killer. Is that really what you're supposed to do?"

"That's what he hired me for."

He said, "To find *the* killer, or to find *a* killer?"

"I'm not supposed to frame anybody, if that's what you're driving at."

"That's where I'm driving," he said. "But I'll tell you someplace I didn't drive, and that's Pennsylvania on Wednesday night. I'm one hundred percent covered. So if what you're down here for is to fit me for the box, forget it."

"How do you know you're covered?"

"I was at a kind of party, it lasted all night."

142

"What do you mean, a kind of party?"

"Like I said."

"You mean a pot party?"

He grinned. "Boy, you are old. How were things at Valley Forge?"

"Cold," I said. "But why are you telling me all these things?"

"I already explained that."

"No you didn't. You told me why it didn't matter whether you talked or not, but you didn't say why you chose to talk."

He took his time with his answer to this one, too, drumming the table top some more and watching his fingers move. When at last he did speak he kept on watching his fingers. He said, "Rita and I had a thing. You know? Sex was a lot of it, what the hell, we both had it better with each other than with anybody else. Anybody else. But that wasn't the whole thing. We were . . . involved, you know? Hung up on each other."

I said, "If it's that tough to say you loved her, just move on. I've got the idea."

He snuck a quick look at my face, then studied his fingers again. "Whatever you want to call it," he said. "It wasn't over, for either one of us. But she needed . . . more. Down here, this was no way for her, she didn't dig this kind of life at all. Cockroaches and all this garbage, poor all the goddamn time, she figured later for that. And I couldn't do it, you know? I couldn't give her all that other stuff."

He looked directly at me now, pleading in a way to be understood. "I'm still me," he said. "You know what I mean? No matter how much I was hung on Rita, I'm still who I am, I've still got to work things out my own way. Right?"

"You mean, you couldn't turn yourself around into somebody who made a lot of money."

"Boy, I thought about it, I really thought about it. I

worked out schemes, I went for job interviews, I did this, I did that, but I just couldn't cut it. I got okayed on some of those jobs, ten, twelve grand a year, and I just couldn't do the bit. I never showed up for the first day, not once." He smiled painfully. "Man, I'm blackballed in every employment agency in town. They won't send me anywhere." Then he shrugged and said, "Besides, ten grand a year wouldn't do it. Not the way Rita wanted to live. In the rack Rembek couldn't compete at all, but how much time can you spend in the rack?"

"All right," I said. "I've got the picture. But you were going to tell me why you're giving it to me."

"Because maybe you're straight," he said. "Maybe you are out to find out who killed her."

"And you want him found."

"You bet your life."

"Well," I said, "I am straight. But that doesn't help much. Because Ernie Rembek didn't kill Rita."

He looked at me with mistrust and scorn. "Is that right?"

"He's covered just as much as you are. I've already checked him out."

"Why should I believe you?"

"Why should either of us believe the other? You're the first one to say to me anything about Rembek planning to marry Rita. Why didn't he tell me himself?"

"Ask him."

"I'm asking you. Is this marriage something you stuck in for effect, because you hate Rembek?"

He was about to give me an angry answer, and reconsidered. "No," he said. "I see what you mean, but no. It's what Rita told me, and that's straight."

"Then maybe she was lying. Did she often?"

"That kind of lie? No. What's the point of it?"

"If not that kind of lie, what kind did she tell?"

"She had Rembek convinced she always had a six-day period." He grinned at the thought and said, "Man, that would have been a marriage. That marriage would have gone down in history, man."

"In other words, she told lies when they had some use."

"Strictly."

"Maybe she wanted you to get on the stick and take one of those ten-grand jobs."

"Who, me? No, man, that isn't the way Rita and I had it. She knew who I was and I knew who she was. You know who paid my rent the last two years?"

"Rita?"

"That's one way to look at it. I figure Mister Ernest Rembek paid it."

"How often did she come down to see you?"

"I don't know, maybe once a month, sometimes more. She couldn't get away very much."

"How did she travel?"

"By cab, what else?"

"Was there anybody else she visited?"

"Well, we had friends down—Oh. You mean, like sex?"

"Yes."

He shook his head. "That isn't what she was. Don't get Rita wrong, mister, she wasn't a whore."

"I already know that. So there were two men in her life, you and Rembek, and that was it."

"Definitely."

"Who did she go with—do you mind the phrase?"

"Okay," he said, grinning. "Okay, you win."

"Fine. Who did she go with before you?"

"Some guy named, uh, Bob something. Like Kearny, Kellogg, some name like that."

"Do you know where he lives?"

145

"Out on the Coast someplace. He went out to LA years ago, he's an actor, he was in a TV series out there."

"In other words, he's long since out of Rita's life."

"Oh, sure. He was out of her life when I came in."

"All right." I offered him a cigarette, which he refused, then lit one for myself. There was no ashtray around, so I had to drop the match on the floor. Then I said, "How dedicated was Rita to her career as an actress?"

"She was big on it," he said. "Really tripped on it. I mean, once Rembek came along she didn't have to do the bit any more, but she still did."

I said, "So far as you've told me, you were important to her, Rembek was important to her because of the money and influence he could give her, and now you say acting was important to her."

He nodded. "Right. That's got her down, those were the three."

"Which was most important?"

"No telling," he said. "Sometimes, me. Sometimes she'd call me up, she couldn't get away and she wanted me bad, and she'd talk me halfway up the wall. Sometimes there wasn't anything in the world but Mister Ernest Rembek and all the good things he could do for her. And if she had a part in something, some play or something on television, the whole world could go to hell, she wasn't interested. I can remember trying to get her into bed sometimes when she'd want to study lines or like that, she'd cut me to pieces."

I said, "She wouldn't have been able to treat Rembek that way."

"She could get around him," he said. "She had him pretty well under control."

I said, "If she was really running away from Rembek, she was also running away from any kind of acting career, be-

146

cause Rembek would have been looking for her."

He shrugged. "If that's what she did, that's what she did."

I said, "Almost nothing you've told me fits in with what I've already got."

"I told you nothing but the truth," he said.

"I believe you, that's the funny part of it. But it could still be that you didn't know Rita as well as you think. Knowing a woman's body doesn't necessarily mean you know her mind."

"I knew Rita," he said. "I'm sure of that much."

"Why would she run away from an acting career?"

"I don't know. Something else came along, maybe."

"Another man?"

He didn't like the thought, but he was feeling some sort of compulsion to be honest with me. He said, "Maybe. In the first flush, maybe. A lot of things seem possible when you're just starting."

"When was the last time you saw her?"

"About three weeks ago. Rembek took her to some kind of play opening and a party afterwards. He got stinko and passed out at her place and she quick came down to spend a couple hours with me."

"What about Robin?"

"I keep my own place. Anyway, I did."

"You mean you don't any more?"

"Not after the first of the month, man. Nobody's around to pay the rent any more. Besides, there's no reason to have my own place now. I'm moving in with Robin."

I said, "Did she say anything to you about a new man she'd met, anybody she was having an affair with or thinking about having an affair with?"

"No, sir, not a one."

"Would she have?"

"I think so. We didn't have sexual secrets from each other."

"Did you ever go up to see her at her place?"

"Not me. The doorman up there would have passed the word on to Rembek."

I said, "Some of the people I've talked to described her as a dumb bunny. What do you say about that?"

He smiled in reminiscent pleasure, saying, "Yeah, I know about that. That was a put-on, you know? Strictly a put-on for the squares."

"Did she put Rembek on that way?"

"Sure. That was the whole basis she had going with him. She could run circles around him and he never knew it." He chuckled and shook his head. "What a marriage that would have been!"

"Can you think of any reason she might have lied to you about marrying Rembek?"

"No. Why should she lie?"

"That's what I want to know. All right, thank you, I guess that's it."

As I was saying that, along came the woman proprietor with our coffee and tea, explaining it had taken so long because she'd had to boil the water, whatever that meant. I offered to pay her, for my earlier coffee and this new round, and the bill was two dollars. I paid it, and left a quarter tip.

Ted Quigley had seen me react to the bill—two dollars for three coffees and a tea was a little high—and grinned, saying, "You pay for the atmosphere in here, man."

"I didn't realize I'd ordered atmosphere. All right, thanks again."

I got to my feet, leaving the new coffee undrunk, and Quigley looked up at me, saying, "I wonder if you could do me a favor."

"If I can."

"It's a funny thing. I don't have any pictures of Rita. Would you believe it? I figure, doing what you're doing, you must have some pictures of her. Would you send me one? I'll give you Robin's address."

I said, "Are you sure that's a good idea, Ted? She really is gone, you know."

His face distorted. "Oh, Jesus," he said. He turned away.

I went up front, to where Robin was sitting, watching me suspiciously, not drinking the tea I'd bought for her. I leaned over in front of her, resting my hand on the table, and said softly, "Ted's working out some grief right now. If I were you, I'd leave him alone for maybe fifteen minutes, and then I'd go get him and take him home and give him the goddamnedest lay of his life."

I left her blinking.

20

Back at Rembek's apartment Roger Kerrigan told me my appointment with William Pietrojetti was for three o'clock and with Matthew Seay for three-thirty. I typed up a quick summary of my meeting with Ted Quigley, filed it, and left with Kerrigan to see my last two suspects.

What I had been told by Quigley changed things, though I as yet had no way of knowing how much. I was sure he had been telling me the truth to the extent that he knew the truth, but I was not entirely convinced that he had fully known the truth. Still, I was prepared to believe that Rita Castle had maintained a fitful sort of relationship with Quigley all the time she was being kept by Ernie Rembek and I was further prepared to believe the implication that the incessant flirtation among Rembek's friends had merely been, along with the dumb-bunny routine, a part of the mocking façade, the "put-on" she had maintained to help her survive the rigors of her relationship with Rembek.

But what was this business about marriage? Rita Castle had told Quigley that Rembek planned to marry her, and so far there didn't seem to be any reason for her to have been lying. But Rembek had made it plain he intended to stay with the wife he already had, and there didn't seem to be any reason for him to be lying either. But one of them must be, must have been. Which one, and why?

I spent most of my time on the trip out to Pietrojetti's

house gnawing on this question without getting any nourishment from it, sitting silent and preoccupied in the back of the limousine with Kerrigan, Dominic Brono once again at the wheel. We drove in the rain out the Long Island Expressway, past the big bulky building where Joseph Lydon stood and sipped at his drink and stared at his view, on out past the city line and eventually to Mineola, one of the endless array of miniature towns packed shoulder to shoulder across the island just beyond Queens.

Pietrojetti lived in a house that looked something like mine on a street that looked very much like mine. The out-of-place limousine pulled to a stop in front of it, Kerrigan and I got out, and Pietrojetti met us at the door.

I had no real expectation that either Pietrojetti or Matthew Seay would turn out to be the man I was after. The death of Mickey Hansel made it plain that I had already touched the killer, that he was more than likely one of the people I'd talked to yesterday. I was going through with these last two interviews partly because in such matters I'm a completist, partly because there was still the vague possibility that one of these two might be my man after all, but mostly because I hoped one or both of them would in the course of the interview say something useful or enlightening.

I had assumed that Pietrojetti was a bachelor, I don't know why, but his house contained a wife, a slender wraith hovering in the background, apron-clad, nervously playing with her fingers, watching and listening, creeping forward slightly when called by Pietrojetti to be introduced. He gave her no name, presenting her to us merely as "My wife." Then, the introductions over, she turned with clear relief and vanished.

Pietrojetti collected clocks, and the house was alive with their ticking. From a grandfather's clock in the hall, its pen-

dulum swinging slowly back and forth in stately contempla-
tion of the passage of time, through a Seth Thomas
mantelpiece clock in the living room, which rang out the
sound of the Westminster chimes every quarter-hour, to a
small and ornate and gilt-encrusted antique clock on an end
table, there were clocks everywhere, all working and all
telling the exact same time.

The three of us sat in the living room, beneath the rustle
and stride of all those clocks. I said, "You have quite a collection here."

He shrugged. "I suppose so," he said, making it clear he
wasn't anxious to talk to me about his hobby.

Well, he was right. I said, "When was the first time you
met Rita Castle?"

"When Mister Rembek brought her to the office. The first
time he brought her. He wanted me to set up the financial arrangements."

"You mean paying the rent?"

He nodded. "And so on," he said

"And so on?"

"Well, there were certain charge accounts, and a weekly
cash outlay for miscellaneous expenses, and so on. All of this
had to be handled in a somewhat roundabout fashion, to
make it deductible."

"You mean tax deductible?"

"Yes. Business expenditures."

"Business expenditures. When was the last time you saw
Miss Castle?"

"Approximately six weeks ago."

"Where was that?"

"She came to the office. There were some papers for her to
sign. She was on the books as an employee, there were occasionally forms to be filled out or papers to be signed."

"Did you ever see her at a party or anything like that?"

He shook his head, smiling thinly. "Oh, no. Janice and I rarely attend parties. We're more the homebody type."

Janice came in at that point, bringing a tray on which, astonishingly enough, there were three glasses of milk and a plate of homemade cookies. She placed this tray silently and deferentially on a coffee table accessible to us all, and then as silently hurried out again, not seeming to hear the confused and mumbled thanks that Kerrigan and I sent after her.

One can do nothing with hospitality but accept it. We all took time out now to munch on cookies—peanut butter, and very good—and drink milk. When a sufficient time had elapsed, I said, "In other words, you never did see Rita Castle in a social situation."

"Not directly, no," he said. "Now and again I was called to Miss Castle's apartment to meet Mister Rembek there for a business discussion, and usually Miss Castle would also be present. Not at the discussion, of course, she would stay elsewhere in the apartment while we talked."

"The money she took away with her," I said. "How much was it?"

He looked for help from Kerrigan, who told him, "It's all right, give him the figure."

"Yes, sir." He turned back to me and said, "Approximately eighty thousand dollars."

"How is it she had access to the cash?"

"It was kept in her apartment. Mister Rembek had a bad experience with a safety deposit box one time—the government obtained a court order to open it—so since that time he has kept his miscellaneous funds in caches at various points, including Miss Castle's apartment."

"Where was it kept?"

"I wouldn't know."

153

"How much did Miss Castle cost Rembek every year?"

He thought about it, and said, "Approximately eleven thousand dollars. That's a very approximate figure, of course."

"In other words, when she left she took about seven years' salary with her."

Beside me Kerrigan chuckled, but Pietrojetti took the question seriously, gazing into the middle distance and saying, "Well, it wouldn't have any legal basis. Of course, if one could arrange prior paperwork a portion of the substance could be written off as a settlement upon severance, and then divert funds from—"

"Well, that's for you to work out," I said, interrupting him, bringing him back to reality. "About Miss Castle's charge accounts. Did she do an unusual amount of spending in the week or two before leaving?"

"Not that I recall," he said. "I've closed off those accounts, of course, and received the final bills, and as I remember them, none of them struck me at the time as unusual or excessive. Of course, I could look into it further for you at the office if you—"

"No, that's all right. What about cash? Did she ask for any extra money in the last few weeks?"

"No, I don't believe so. I think I would have noticed, I'd remember it."

"All right." I got to my feet. "Thank you for your time."

"Not at all."

"And thank your wife for the, uh, milk and cookies. It was a pleasant surprise."

In his thin way, he showed pleasure and embarrassed confusion, thanking me for my thanks, preceding us to the door. His wife was nowhere in evidence. We left and walked through the rain back to the limousine and headed again for Manhattan.

In the car, Kerrigan looked at me and said, "You surprise me, Mister Tobin."

"Why's that?"

"You handle yourself well in a comic situation. I didn't think you would."

"I live in a house like that," I said. "On a street like that."

"Don't kid me, Mister Tobin," said Kerrigan.

21

Matthew Seay was a hobbyist too, but of a different and more subtle kind. His apartment on Riverside Drive in Manhattan was furnished in a somewhat unusual fashion, the significance of which I failed at first to understand, so that I spent unnecessary time with him.

On the trip back from Long Island, Kerrigan had told me several things about Seay, not including the central fact, which he himself at that time didn't know. What he had told me was that Seay was a strong-arm man and bodyguard on general call in the corporation. That is, he wasn't specifically any one person's bodyguard, but was assigned to certain individuals at special times. He was what Kerrigan called a "show guard," which is to say he could be shown in public, he was a bodyguard who could accompany his master into any social or public situation without looking out of place.

Kerrigan was right about that. Seay met us at the door, wearing a black suit, black tie, black shoes and silver accessories, looking like the prototype movie idol, a tall, big-shouldered, narrow-waisted, blond-haired, strong-jawed, handsome and smiling Adonis, a kind of trim weight-lifter, the ultimate lifeguard on the beach. No one would object to this man's presence, not at a formal reception, an after-theater party, anywhere. No one would suspect him of being anything so crude as a syndicate hoodlum's bodyguard.

Smiling, welcoming us with a radio announcer's voice,

Seay ushered us into the living room, a bright large room full of spidery antiques plus two very old plush sofas, one green and one orange. Paintings of sad-looking clowns hung on the walls, statuettes of muscular men were placed here and there on pedestals and small tables, a number of candelabra were scattered about, and crossed swords gleamed on the wall above the fireplace.

Seay asked us if we would have drinks, which we both declined, and then we all sat down to begin, Seay on the green sofa, me on the orange, and Kerrigan on one of the spidery chairs off to one side.

I said, "You know what we're here about, don't you?"

"I believe I do," he said. "Miss Rita Castle." He spoke in an overly precise way, clipping off the ends of his words, an extreme carefulness about being understood that implied condescension, though there was otherwise no sign of condescension in his manner.

I said, "I suppose you saw Miss Castle mostly in the course of your work."

He nodded gravely. "Yes. Whilst escorting Mister Rembek."

Whilst! I was taken aback at the word, losing the thread for just a second, until I saw out of the corner of my eye Kerrigan not entirely suppressing a grin, which helped me get back on the track. I said, "Did you ever meet or see Rita Castle when Ernie Rembek *wasn't* around?"

"Oh, no," he said, smiling politely. "I know them both only in my official capacity. Knew them? It's difficult to know which verb to use."

I wasn't going to be thrown off any more. I said, "What was Miss Castle's attitude toward you, generally speaking?"

"Oh, quite pleasant," he said, with the same polite smile.

"We had one or two conversations on fashion and whatnot."

"You liked her?"

"Well, of course she was of a type, hardly an individual, but rather a pleasant example of the mode. I enjoyed chatting with her."

"Were there ever any . . . overtures between you?"

"Overtures?" He seemed totally blank for an instant, and then smiled like sunshine breaking through the clouds. "Oh, you mean sex! Oh, no, not a bit. Rita Castle? Not for an instant."

"You mean you didn't," I suggested.

"Well, neither of us," he said, and made a shrugging gesture. "Why should we? I daresay we understood one another."

It was more than I was managing to do. Something about Matthew Seay was clamoring for my attention, and I couldn't think what it was. Something about the way he furnished his room, something . . .

I said, "Would you mind if I looked around your apartment? Without touching anything."

"But of course."

He started to rise, but I said, "I'd rather go by myself, if it's all right with you."

He settled again. "Certainly," he said, and made a gracious motion toward the inner door, offering me the run of the place.

As I left the living room he was offering Kerrigan a drink again, and Kerrigan was refusing it.

A cream-walled hallway led deeper into the apartment past several abstract paintings. The kitchen was large and airy, with curtains on the windows, a great number of copper-bottomed pots hung on hooks along the wall above the stove, and a general air of tidiness and constant use. The bathroom had burlap-covered walls and a painting of a horse above the toilet. But it was in the bedroom that I came to my belated understanding.

The bedroom was all purple plush, dominated by a huge canopied double bed with dark draperies all around. I opened the draperies on one side, found a purple bedspread within, and purple pillows. The underside of the canopy was a great dark mirror.

Beside the bed was a bookcase, small and dark tight-packed with a jumbled and dog-eared collection of male physique magazines and nudist magazines. Atop a massive dresser were a great number of perfume bottles, all opened and partly used.

A white telephone on the bookcase rang once.

I opened the closet door and found the clothing separated down the middle into two distinct groupings. On the left were the suits and jackets and slacks to be expected of a man in Seay's social and occupational position, but on the right were a great number of costumes. Leopard skins, leotards. Batman and Satan. A wedding gown, a nun's habit. A pirate, a spaceman, and Mickey Mouse.

From the doorway behind me Seay's voice said, calmly, "A phone call for you, Mister Tobin."

I shut the closet door and turned to face him, seeing him standing there with a faint smile on his face. It pleased him to have been found out. When next he came in here he would remember my face; I didn't much care for that.

I said, "A very interesting array."

"Thank you."

"You have said you spent Wednesday night with a friend, but you wouldn't give any details."

He nodded, the small smile still flickering about his lips. "Quite so."

I went over to the bed, pulled a drape open, and motioned at the mirror up above. "Was that the friend?"

He smiled like a Cupid; his mouth seemed wet. He said, "You may take the call on that phone there if you wish."

I closed the drape again. "Thank you."

He left the doorway, as silently as he had come, and I went over to the white telephone and picked it up and said hello.

Ernie Rembek's voice spoke, with a background of jumbled noise as though a great number of men were talking. He said, "Is that you, Mister Tobin?"

"Yes, speaking."

"Hold on, let me close this door."

I listened to the jumbled noise, and then to silence, and then to his voice again, saying, "There, that's better. You still there?"

"Yes."

"Well, you better come back double fast."

"What's the matter?"

"Remember Paul Einhorn? The one that ran away."

"With the father and two uncles in Florida. Yes, I remember. What about him?"

"The cops just found him dead."

"Where? How?"

"Hotel room, 46th Street. Shot in the head."

"I want what they have," I said. "Before they have it, I want it. I'll be right there."

"It'll be waiting," he promised.

22

Rembek's apartment was full of people, all men, all formally dressed in dark suits, standing around in small groups, talking together in low tones, most of them holding drinks in their hands. It looked like the lobby of a convention hotel, but more serious.

Rembek met us just inside the front door, saying, "I'm still waiting on the call."

"I'll be in my office," I said. "Come along, Kerrigan."

We went on through the crowd, and when we got into my office with the door shut I said, "What is all that out there?"

He shrugged. "A sort of wake," he said. "An expression of sympathy from the boys."

"A wake? Without a body?"

"Rita's parents had her shipped back to South Dakota," he said. "Ernie checked with them and found out they were having a wake for her today and the burial tomorrow. So he thought he'd have a wake here, too. Sort of an expression of, uhhh, respect. And loss."

I'd seen this absurd sentimentality in the underworld before, but in this particular instance I found it startling. True enough the girl was dead, but before dying she had run out on Rembek in a very harsh way, and had left behind her a note couched in terms of calculated cruelty. Still, I supposed it was understandable that Rembek's memory would prefer to hurdle that recent history and concentrate its attention instead on the more pleasant parts of the past.

If Quigley had been telling the truth, of course, about Rita's attitude toward Rembek—if he had known the truth about it—then this mock wake was after all a very grotesque and ugly joke.

Kerrigan said, "If you don't mind, Mister Tobin, I believe I'll go out and circulate a little. Put in an appearance."

"In a minute," I said. "I want to talk to you first."

"About what?"

"About the fact that you're my number one suspect," I said.

That shook him, for just a second. He said, "Oh. Well, uhhh, well. I didn't know I was doing that good."

"Let's look at the list," I said. I went over and sat down at the desk and began to write out the names again, commenting on each as I went along. Kerrigan stood beside me and watched the names emerge from the pencil.

"With Einhorn dead," I said, "I've got six possibles. Of them all, Pietrojetti is in my opinion the least likely. He knew about the money, but he just doesn't fit as someone Rita Castle would call a 'real man.' Besides, if he wanted to steal eighty thousand dollars I'm sure he could do it easiest and fastest with a pen and a ledger. This isn't his kind of plot."

Kerrigan nodded. "Least likely," he said. "I'll go along with that."

"I'll put Donner next," I said, "because I have to believe him when he says he hasn't looked at another woman in twenty-eight years. Also because he's nearly as unlikely as Pietrojetti to be called a 'real man' by Rita Castle."

"Fine," said Kerrigan. "I'm still with you."

"Lydon third from the bottom," I said. "He's got youth going for him, and an unhappy home life. But a man in real estate in this city, with as many holdings as Lydon, doesn't have to get this complicated if he wants quick money. Besides, I think he's a whiner and I think Rita Castle would have felt immediate contempt for him and nothing would ever have made her change her opinion."

"Nobody looks likely so far," said Kerrigan. "And I'm still agreeing with everything you say."

"That's the bottom half of the list," I said. "The upper three are all much likelier. Third from the top is Louis Hogan. It's entirely possible he's of a type she might have considered a real man, and that incident he told us, about 'inspecting' her in his garage when her flirtation irritated him, just might have been the sort of thing to intrigue her. He's a union executive, which means he wouldn't necessarily have any other way to get a lot of money fast if he needed it, and so might be forced to resort to something like this. He also seems like the sort of man who might live beyond his income."

Kerrigan said, "Why isn't he at the top of the list?"

"Because I have trouble believing he could have fooled Rita Castle about his motives. She was a very complicated girl herself, full of false faces and deceptions, and I think it would require a complicated and artful man to pull the wool over her eyes. Hogan strikes me as too blunt a personality."

Kerrigan said, "You may be right. But you left somebody off that list. Hogan should be number two, at least. In fact, everybody should come up one notch."

"Why?"

"Because Seay ought to go at the bottom."

"Why's that?"

"Isn't it obvious? Because he's a faggot."

I shook my head. "No, he isn't, not exactly. I suppose he does take other men to bed from time to time, but only as surrogates for himself. No, the kind he is he might very well be capable of playing the heterosexual game with a great deal of competence, if the reason was compelling enough."

"If you say so," he said doubtfully.

I said, "Matthew Seay carries beyond sane limits several tendencies which I think were also present—to a lesser degree—in Rita Castle. It's entirely possible she would have been attracted to someone who would seem to have such a deep instinctive understanding of her. The picture of the two of them together has a certain nightmarish rightness to it."

Kerrigan laughed. "A pair of false faces talking to each other."

The image that had come into my own mind was similar to that, but worse. I suddenly saw Rita Castle and Matthew Seay as a pair of puppeteers, hidden in darkness from one another, operating by means of long white strings two marionettes down below. The marionettes posture before one another, dance together, make love, and all the while up rises the faint clacking sounds of the wooden joints.

Does the male marionette strike the female down, crush its wooden skull, leave it bleeding straw alone on the little stage?

I shook my head. Such imagery had too narrow an application, it wouldn't help me to the answer I needed.

Kerrigan said, "Anyway, that leaves only me, right at the top."

"Yes." I wrote his name above the others. "You're the likeliest."

"Could I ask why?"

"You're single, and therefore most readily available to have an affair. You have the youth and self-confidence and style to potentially be Rita Castle's real man. You are smart enough to have set this thing up, and you're probably devious enough, too. I doubt your job leaves openings for making a lot of money quickly, the way Pietrojetti's does, and at the same time I think it possible you would live beyond your means. Particularly if you got involved with someone like Rita Castle."

He gave me a thin smile and said, "It's a persuasive case. What are you going to do now?"

"I'm not entirely persuaded of it yet," I said, "so I'm not going to say anything right now to Rembek." I put the pencil down, leaned back, and studied Kerrigan's face. "If I were still on the force," I said, "at this point I'd have you picked up for questioning. I'd make sure we could hold onto you for a minimum of fifteen hours, I'd set up shifts of teams to question you, and I'd see if there was anything interesting inside your head."

He nodded, smiling sardonically. "I know the style," he said. "I'd come through it, Mister Tobin, smelling like a rose. And it wouldn't prove a thing."

"But it's what I would do," I said. "It's what I think of as the next step. But the way things are, I'll have to find a different next step."

"Do you have any ideas?"

"Some. I want you to help me."

He spread his hands, half jokingly. "Whatever you want, Mister Tobin," he said. "All you have to do is name it."

"I'd like you to prove two things to me," I said. I counted them off on my fingers. "First, I'd like you to prove to me that your emotional life the last few months has been so satisfactory that you wouldn't have started an affair with Rita Castle or anybody else under any circumstances at all. Second, I'd like you to prove to me that your financial condition is absolutely sound, that you have all the money you need for expenses, that you have adequate savings, and that neither in the present nor in the foreseeable future is there any economic crisis in store for you."

He smiled sadly, shaking his head. "I'm sorry, Mister Tobin," he said, "but it can't be done."

"Neither?"

"Neither," he agreed. "First of all, my emotional life, as you call it, is a mess. I'm still emotionally involved with my ex-wife, if you want the truth, and I've been trying to cure it with fast doses of this girl, that girl, the other girl. If I'd thought Rita really meant it when she tossed me the high-sign, I probably would have taken her up on it, because that's the way I'm working it these days. I keep thinking one of them will have the antidote."

"That's the emotional side," I said. "What about the financial?"

"You made a good guess about me before," he said. "I've been just slightly overextended for about the last nine years. It's no worse than usual now, but it's no better either. My ex-wife comes into this part, too; she gets very generous alimony."

I said, "Then you can't do anything to help me get your name farther down the list?"

"I can only tell you Rita never gave me a signal that I could believe in. Therefore there was no affair, and therefore I didn't kill her."

"We'll have to work on it some more," I said.

He said, "What makes you hesitate, Mister Tobin? Why not just turn me over to Ernie? He's got teams of questioners, too, they could maybe cover even more ground than your kind in fifteen hours."

"I won't do that unless I'm sure."

"Why aren't you sure?"

I said, "If you killed Rita Castle, you also booby-trapped my other office, which means you want me dead. So far today

I've given you four good shots at killing me and you haven't taken a one of them."

"Well, I'll be damned," he said. Then he said, "What if I *had* taken one of them?"

"One of us would be dead now, I suppose."

Before he could answer, the door burst open and Rembek came striding in, smiling broadly, saying, "Well, that wraps it up! It's all over, Mister Tobin, it just came over the phone."

I said, "What just came over the phone?"

"Suicide," he said. "Paul Einhorn killed himself." He turned to Kerrigan, saying, "See how it works? Paul's the one who killed Rita, that's why he ran away. But he knew we were on him, that's why he rigged the bomb, and that's why he killed himself." To me he said, "You can hear it for yourself, Mister Tobin, my man's still on the wire."

I looked at Kerrigan. "Now I'm persuaded," I said.

23

Rembek frowned at us both. "What is this?"

Kerrigan said to me, "Let me tell it."

"Go ahead."

"Thank you," he said, and nodded his head at me. Calm as ever, he turned to Rembek. "Mister Tobin has the idea I'm the one. We were just talking about it, how I'm the number one suspect but he wasn't quite sure yet, he wasn't one hundred percent persuaded."

Rembek was frowning harder and harder, glaring at both of us. He said to me, "Is this on the level?"

"Yes."

Kerrigan said, "Now that Paul's dead, he's sure." He turned his head and looked at me. "Aren't you, Mister Tobin?"

I said, "It depends how Einhorn died."

Rembek spread his hands, saying, "What's that mean? I just told you, he shot himself."

I said, "Maybe."

Kerrigan wasn't being cocky about the situation but at the same time he didn't seem particularly ruffled by it either. He said to Rembek, "The way Mister Tobin sees it, maybe Paul didn't shoot himself at all. Maybe he was shot by somebody else and the thing set up to look like suicide. And if that's what happened, he figures the somebody that did it is me."

Rembek said, to both of us, "Why?"

I said, "Let Kerrigan tell it, he's doing fine."

Kerrigan didn't smile. He said to me, "It's not that hard to figure, Mister Tobin. I always admitted the thing was plausible."

"Tell it to me," said Rembek.

Kerrigan told it to him: "I've got money troubles. Not bad, but chronic. And I've got woman trouble because of my ex-wife. So there's my two motives. I've got as much opportunity as anybody else, and Mister Tobin figures I might fit that 'real man' line in Rita's note."

Rembek said, "What's this got to do with Paul?"

"The way Mister Tobin sees it," Kerrigan explained, "when he and I went to see Paul, I took Paul to one side and talked him into making a run for it. Then I arranged for Paul to call me later, I went to see him, killed him, and set it up to look like a suicide."

"Why?"

"To make him take the rap. You came in here yourself, Ernie, saying it was all wrapped up."

Rembek had slowly backed up until he blocked the door. Now, standing there, he looked grimly at me and said, "Is that the way you read it? Did he tell it right?"

"Yes."

He turned back to Kerrigan. "What do you say?"

"I say I didn't do it."

I said, "Let me hear about Einhorn. Can I take it on this phone?"

"Press the button for 72."

I did, and picked up the receiver and said, "You still there?"

A guarded voice said, "Who is this?"

I said, "You're supposed to tell me about the Einhorn homicide."

"Suicide."

"Details."

He said, "Body found in room 516, Warrington Hotel, 290 West 47th Street. He'd taken the room last night, one-ten A.M., using the name Paul Standish. No luggage. About twelve-thirty this afternoon the maid came around to clean the room. She knocked on the door, heard the shot, used her key on—"

"Wait a second," I said. "Give me that sequence again. She knocked on the door before the shot?"

"Right. As soon as she knocked he shot himself. She opened the door right away and—"

"She didn't go after the manager?"

"Definitely no. She went straight in, found him on the floor, and called the desk from the room phone."

"Is there a ledge outside the window?"

"No. And no connecting rooms. It's suicide, no question. He held the gun to the side of his head and pulled the trigger. His head has the marks of a contact wound, his hand passes the paraffin test, his prints are on the gun."

I didn't like giving it up. I said, "Where was the gun? In his hand?"

"On the floor beside the body, where it dropped."

"Hold on a second," I said. "Let me think."

"Take your time," he said.

Rembek and Kerrigan were watching me, Rembek grimly and Kerrigan warily. I closed my eyes against their eyes and thought.

It did make sense as a suicide, I had to admit it. Einhorn had simply run away for the last time. He must have been sure his father and uncles would drag him back home to Florida, maybe for good, and this time it was just too much. So he got himself a gun—a gun is as easy to buy in New York as a pack of razor blades—and sat in his room thinking about killing himself, and probably thinking sometimes about killing his

170

father and uncles instead or as well, and when the knock had sounded at the door he'd assumed it was the pursuit, catching up with him, and he put the gun to his head and pulled the trigger.

All right.

I opened my eyes. I said into the phone, "Who are you?"

He said, "That isn't part of the deal."

"How do I know this information is trustworthy?"

"It's the goods," he said.

"Are you on the force?"

"That isn't part of the deal," he said, and hung up.

I held the phone away from my ear and said to Rembek "How much can I count on this man?"

"He's on the scene," Rembek told me. "You can take his word one hundred percent."

"Then it's suicide," I said, and cradled the phone. I noticed the look of relief that washed quickly across Kerrigan's face, to be replaced just as quickly by his usual expression of unruffled calm.

Rembek said to me, "Does that take Roger off the hook?"

"Off the hook," I said, "but not off the list."

Rembek had been keyed up to take vengeance and he was having trouble throttling back. He didn't quite look at Kerrigan as he said, gruffly, "All right. I'll be outside if you want me."

"What about the police records on my suspects?"

"Oh," he said. "With all this other stuff, I forgot. Top drawer of your filing cabinet, manila envelope."

"Good. Thank you."

He left, and Kerrigan said, "Are you done with me now?"

"Yes. Is Rembek's lawyer out there?"

"Which one, Canfield?"

"Yes. If he's there, I want—no, wait a second. Rembek's

got more than one lawyer?"

"Sure. He's got two. Canfield's a corporation attorney, he isn't Ernie's personal lawyer."

I said, "I wish I'd known that before. All right, who's the personal attorney?"

"Sam Goldberg. He was one of the men with alibis from your first list."

"Is he here?"

"I don't know. He might be."

"I want to talk to him," I said.

"I'll take a look," he said, and went out.

While I waited, I looked at the record sheets on my six suspects. They made pretty reading.

Kerrigan, as he'd told me in our first interview, had no civilian record at all. But he did have an Army court-martial, and stockade time, having been found guilty of assaulting an officer. There were no details given.

Matthew Seay had a number of arrests, all in the mid-fifties, three times for possession of narcotics, once for contributing to the delinquency of a male minor, once for beating up a sailor in a West Side bar, once for automobile theft, twice for possession and sale of pornographic materials. His most recent arrest was seven years old and he had never served any jail time, though he'd been given a number of suspended sentences.

Louis Hogan, as he'd told me, had no record at all.

Joseph Lydon had two arrests and no convictions, the first arrest being on a Sullivan Law charge, carrying of a concealed weapon, and the second an assault charge growing out of a fight with a tenant in one of his buildings.

Frank Donner had the longest record of them all, but with only two jail terms, one in the early thirties for assault with a deadly weapon and one in the late forties for blackmail and forgery. His other arrests, some with no convictions and some with suspended sentences, ranged from bribery and extortion to arson and assault. His last twelve years had been free of arrests of any kind.

William Pietrojetti had two arrests, two convictions, and two jail terms, the first in 1947 for tax fraud and the second in 1952 for receiving stolen property.

The six dossiers made a grim picture, but I knew they told far less than the whole story. This was the visible fraction of the iceberg; beneath the surface lay all the crimes for which these six men had never received any official notice at all.

In one way of looking at things, I could point at any one of these men, turn him over to Rembek to be dealt with, and rest easy with the knowledge that the punishment he got would be due him for *something* in his life even if not for the murder of Rita Castle. I found myself tempted to handle the case just that way; construct a box around Kerrigan, say, or Donner, or Seay, take my five-thousand bonus, and go back to my wall. What difference did it make, really, whether or not the murderer of Rita Castle was ever punished for that crime, with all the unpunished crimes already existing in the world, with all the unpunished crimes stated or implied merely by these six dossiers?

But I couldn't do it. It wasn't any sense of responsibility that held me back, or any desire to see justice done, or even any interest in particular in the task I was out to perform. It was merely that this was my profession, and that it was impossible for me to work at my profession in any other way than with my best efforts. When I handed someone over to the authorities—or to Rembek, depending on the situation— it would be when I was sure I had the right man.

As I was studying the dossiers and thinking about my attitudes to the job, Rembek came back in, saying, "What do you want to see Goldberg for?"

"Stay and listen," I said.

"He's got nothing to do with the corporation," he said. "He's my personal attorney."

"Still," I said, "I have things to ask him."

"You're looking for somebody in the corporation," he insisted. "Sam Goldberg can't help you."

"Rita Castle was a part of your personal life," I explained. "So I want to talk to your personal attorney."

"You don't need him."

"Either I talk to him, or I'm off the case."

"You want to quit? You keep threatening to quit. You really want to quit?"

I did, of course, if I were given the right out, but all I said was, "I do if I don't get to talk to Sam Goldberg."

"Then quit," Rembek said. "Goodbye." And he stalked out, leaving the door open.

24

Kerrigan stopped me at the front door. He wanted to know what was going on, and I told him Rembek had accepted my resignation. He said, "You mean you're on strike?"

"No. I mean I'm going home and I'm not going to think about all this any more."

"You can't."

"I can. Easily."

I left. Down on the sidewalk the doorman tipped his hat at me and called me sir and asked if he should get me a cab. I walked on without acknowledging his presence, went to the subway, and took my train out to Queens.

The house was very empty. I called Kate in Patchogue and told her she could come on home, I'd quit the job. She wanted to know why and I told her it was because my employer had put an obstruction in my path that made it impossible for me to go on. She asked me if that wasn't an excuse, and I said, "Maybe it is, but it doesn't matter, because it's also the truth."

The rain had lessened and was now merely a fine mist, almost hanging suspended in the air. I went out to the backyard, took the tarpaulin off the hole, and started putting down a first layer of concrete block, getting each piece level and smooth and at the proper depth, filling the holes in the blocks with dirt, packing earth in on the sides. I was completely absorbed by the work I was doing, and did no thinking about the murder of Rita Castle.

Two or three times I heard the phone ringing, but I didn't answer.

I worked as long as I could, until it was too dark to see what I was doing, and then reluctantly put the tarp over the hole again and went into the house. Kate and Bill should have been home long before this, so I called Patchogue again and they were still there. Kate said, "I tried to call you, but there wasn't any answer."

"I was in the yard."

"We'll stay over here tonight," she said. "If you still want us to come home tomorrow, we will."

"I'm not going to change my mind," I said.

"I'd rather do it this way," she said.

So we left it at that. I took a shower, made myself an easy dinner, and then sat in the living room with one lamp lit and watched television. There were no more phone calls. At eleven-thirty I went to bed. I was quite tired from my work in the backyard, and fell immediately asleep.

Sunday morning opened cloudy, but without rain. I had a quick breakfast but didn't shave, and was out in the yard by nine o'clock.

They came a little before eleven, Rembek and Kerrigan and a short round white-haired man with round spectacles and a black briefcase. If they rang the front doorbell I didn't hear it, and wasn't aware of them till I looked up from my digging and saw them coming around the corner of the house.

I knew then I'd never believed it would be that easy to get rid of the job. I knew I had always known it would come after me, it would keep coming after me until it was done, until the murderer of Rita Castle was found and punished.

I stood leaning on my shovel and watched them come diagonally across the yard toward me. Rembek and Kerrigan looked around in some surprise at the signs of digging, at the mounds of material, but the third man merely came forward, moving in a sort of dogged roll, like a man grown old and fat in luxury and comfort who has suddenly been thrust outside to make his way amid the nettles as best he can.

The three of them stopped in front of me, and Rembek jabbed a thumb at the third man, saying, "All right, here he is."

I said, without hope, "You accepted my resignation."

It was Kerrigan who answered. "Mister Tobin," he said, "you can consider that when Ernie hired you he was doing so in the name of the corporation. It's the corporation you've been working for, and the corporation hasn't accepted any resignation from you, and isn't going to accept any resignation from you."

"Yes," I said. "Of course." There was no point in further discussion. I put down the shovel and climbed up out of the hole. "If you'll wait for me inside," I said, "I'll get cleaned up."

The third man—he had to be Sam Goldberg, judging by Rembek's nameless introduction—snapped, "I have an appointment at twelve-thirty."

"It's Sunday," Rembek said, in irritation. "What do you want with appointments on Sunday?"

"I didn't want this one either," said Goldberg. He was peppery, for such a round man.

I led them into the house and left them in the living room while I went upstairs to shower and shave. When I came back down, Goldberg said, "Could we get this over as soon as possible?"

"Of course," I said. I sat down and asked him, "How long ago did Rembek come to you about the divorce?"

Kerrigan betrayed his surprise, Rembek's grim mouth told

177

me he'd known this was going to be the subject, and Goldberg, oblivious of any special import to the question, answered it by saying, "About three months ago."

"What's been done on it so far?"

"Paperwork? Nothing."

"Why?"

He made an irritable little shrug, a fat man's shrug, and said, "Ernie's been blowing hot and cold on the subject. One day this, one day that. They told me to speak frankly to you."

"Thank you," I said. "You say he's been blowing hot and cold. Has he come to a final decision at all, do you know?"

"They're all final decisions," he snapped. "Every three days another phone call: yes! no! yes! no! The last word I've heard is no."

In a sad attempt at adult reasonableness, Rembek said, "Sam, you're overstating the case. It wasn't back and forth that much."

But Goldberg was in no mood to help Rembek retain his dignity. Turning on him, he said, "I've told you for months, that girl's made a fool out of you. Every three days another phone call, don't tell me."

I said, "Have you talked it over with Mrs. Rembek?"

Goldberg spread his hands. "How could I? It was never on long enough."

"Did you tell her or did Rembek?"

Rembek shouted angrily, "She doesn't know! Nobody told her, she doesn't know!"

Goldberg gave his little shrug again. "If she knows, it isn't from me."

I said, "I get the impression you didn't care for Rita Castle."

"I prefer not to speak unkindly of the dead."

"Would you tell me what you used to say about her when she was alive?"

He looked at me in some surprise, and an instant later flashed a surprisingly bright and merry smile. "I'd be happy to," he said. "When she was alive, I said of her that she was a cheap golddigger and a tramp and that she had so much contempt for Ernie that she didn't even bother to hide it. I said that she was marrying him for commercial reasons exclusively and that he would live to regret it. I said that if he hadn't promised to put money into this theater operation of hers, she wouldn't have agreed to marry him at all, and I predicted a longer run for the play than the marriage."

I turned to Rembek. "What play?"

"*Hedda Gabler*," he said sullenly. "She wanted to direct."

"Not appear?"

"No. Acting was just interpreting, that's what she said. She wanted to direct."

"And you were going to produce."

"Off-Broadway," he said defensively, as though the smaller budget thus implied was somehow a point in his favor.

"What had been done on it so far?"

"Nothing. We were going to start after—when we—"

"After you were married."

He didn't say anything.

I said, "Why did you lie to me at the beginning? Why tell me the girl wasn't really important to you, why make such a point about your wife not finding out?"

"She was dead," he said. "It was all over. What difference did it make?"

"It confused the issue," I told him. "It wasted my time. It made me struggle to learn things you could have simply given me at the beginning."

He said, "You want the truth? I was ashamed. I'd found out Sam was right about her, everybody was right about her. After I saw that note."

"Yes, the note," I said. "I don't like that note any more than you do." I got to my feet. "I have to go back to Allentown," I said.

25

Rembek insisted on coming along, though I told him there was no point in it, he would see nothing and learn nothing. Still, he came. We let Sam Goldberg off in midtown, went through the Lincoln Tunnel, and the limousine stretched itself out along the road west.

Kerrigan rode in front beside the driver, Dominic Brono. Rembek and I sat in back a great width of seat between us, each of us sunk in his own thoughts. Rembek's, judging from his somber face, were mostly sour thoughts, while mine were optimistic. I didn't know yet who was the inspiration for all this chaos, but at least the lies and confusions and false trails had been cleared away. I was no longer working from inaccurate postulates, and it seemed to me I was very close to the end. Maybe today.

For most of the ride out we were all silent, but at one point I did have a brief conversation with Kerrigan, to which Rembek listened as though in hopes of hearing the word that would save him and restore everything to what it was. What I was asking Kerrigan about was one of the possibilities that had occurred to me, which I found unlikely but which had to be dealt with.

I said, "Kerrigan, the corporation considers Rembek an important man, doesn't it?"

He looked over his shoulder at me. "Of course. He runs a district."

"The corporation might feel protective about him."

He thought about it, not liking the word protective, and finally said, "In a way. They'd like him to go on functioning."

"It occurs to me," I said, "that the corporation might have thought Rita Castle dangerous to Rembek's functioning, and might have had her killed in order to protect his usefulness."

He considered that one, too, and said, "Possibly. It's unlikely, but it is possible."

"What I'm wondering," I said, "is how the corporation would behave now if that were the way it happened. You'd be the man sent to be sure I didn't find out the truth."

He shook his head. "That isn't how we'd do it," he said.

"I'm glad to hear it. How would you do it?"

"Ernie had to ask permission to hire you. If the corporation had eliminated Rita, Ernie would have been told no, there were policy reasons why it was best to let everything lie. He might have been told that anyway, it all depends on the situation in the world."

I turned to Rembek. "If they'd said no, what would you have done?"

"Waited," he said. "Hoped I could do it later on."

"You wouldn't have argued?"

It was Kerrigan who answered. "You don't argue with the corporation," he said.

I said, "All right. Would you have suspected the corporation had killed Rita if they told you no?"

"Of course not," he said. "They didn't have to. If they didn't like Rita they would have come talk to me first."

I looked at Kerrigan. "Is that right?"

He nodded.

"Good," I said. I sat back and removed that possibility from my thoughts.

We ran into drizzling rain at Easton, which had become a

downpour by the time we reached Allentown. It was only one-thirty in the afternoon, but dark enough for most cars to have their headlights on.

The lights of the Mid-Road Motel were also on, red and blue and white neon, suggesting warmth and dryness. Brono pulled the limousine to a stop as close to the office door as possible, and I said, "You all wait here. I won't be long."

"I'll come along," said Kerrigan.

"Don't argue with me," I said.

I got out of the car, took three running steps through the pelting rain, and pushed through the door into the office. MacNeill was there, sitting on a high stool behind the counter, his elbows on the ledger. He'd been gazing out the streaming window at the rain and the road, daydreaming, and he blinked at me in some confusion for a few seconds before reorienting himself. Then he said, "Yes, sir. Room? No weather to travel, is it?"

"You remember me," I said. "I came about the dead girl."

"Oh! Yes, now I do. I'm sorry, I was wool-gathering. What can I do for you?"

"I'd like to speak with your wife," I said.

That confused him again. "Betsy?"

"If you don't mind."

"Oh, no, not at all, not at all." He got down from the stool and headed toward the rear, pausing to mumble, "Scuse. Back in a second."

They came back together and I said to him, "I'd like to speak to Betsy alone for a minute."

"Sure thing," he said hastily, as though someone had accused him of being unco-operative. "Go right ahead, go right ahead." He went through the curtain again and out of sight.

Betsy, as ill-named as ever, stood waiting, as sullen and

truculent as a Sherman tank. I asked her, "Will he listen at the curtain?"

"No," she said, and her lip curled. "He wouldn't think of it. He'll go out to the kitchen."

"Does he know about the money?"

There was no sound for quite a while but the distant drumming of the rain. She stood there unmoved, unchanging, as though nothing had been said to her. Her dress was faded toward gray from its original blue-flower pattern, her apron was totally gray with none of its original color or pattern still showing, her shoes were heavy, laced, low-heeled, scuffed oxfords, she wore gray bobby vex, her shins showed small bites or pimples, and she'd done little or nothing with her hair for quite a while. She stood there looking like something from a photo of Russian peasant women rebuilding a road, and we both listened to the rain and the silence and the echoes of the question I'd asked her.

Finally, hopelessly, she decided to lie. "I don't know what you're talking about."

"Out in the car," I told her, "are Mister Rembek and another important man from the corporation. I haven't told them yet about you taking the money. If I can avoid unnecessary trouble, I'd rather. So I've come in here alone, you'll give me the money, and I won't tell them how I got it."

"I don't know about any money," she said, in a monotone, not really expecting me to believe her.

"If you won't give it to me," I said, "I'll have to tell Rembek so he can have men start searching for it. Then when they find it Rembek will punish you. It's up to you which way you want it."

She went over to the window, walking heavy-legged, and rested a soft thick hand on the sill, and looked out at the rain. "We're going to lose this place," she said. "If we could make

184

it through till summer we'd be okay, but we can't. We won't get through the winter."

"Failure is your way of life," I said. "Don't try to change it."

She turned her head, with puzzled animation in her eyes. "That's a rotten thing to say."

"Bring me the money, Betsy."

She looked away from me, at nothing. We hung there an instant, in that second of stillness at the top of an arc, before the fall down the other side. Then, wordless, she turned back from the window, padded around the counter, and went through the curtain.

She was back a minute later with a black leather bag. She handed it to me, neither of us said anything, and I went back out to the car.

Rembek stared at the bag as I got in. "Where the hell did you get that?"

"I found it."

"*They* took it."

"No," I said. "I found it."

"Where?"

"None of your business," I said.

He glowered out the rainy window toward the office. "They did take it, those two."

I said, "Kerrigan, you heard me say the MacNeills didn't take the money. I don't want any misguided attempts at vengeance on them."

He nodded. "There won't be," he promised.

Rembek said, "Maybe *they* killed her."

I shook my head. "No. The killer's in New York."

"You know who it is?"

"Not yet. Not entirely. But that's where we're going now."

"To the city? Where? Back to my place?"

185

"No. I want to see Frank Donner."

Rembek leaped on the name. "It was Frank? How could it be Frank?"

"It isn't Frank," I told him. "Frank Donner didn't kill Rita, I know that much."

"Then what do you want to see him for?"

"You'll come along when I talk to him," I said. I leaned forward. "All right, Dominic. Back to the city."

"Yes, sir."

We slid like a launch through the rain, the tires hissing, leaving delicate wakes behind them. The space between Rembek and me gradually filled with packets of bills as he counted the money with which the black bag was crammed. No one spoke.

We were nearing Easton before Rembek was finished. Then he announced, "It's a grand short."

Kerrigan turned his head, glanced at me, then said to Rembek, "Forget it."

"Damn it," said Rembek. "A grand short, damn it."

So Betsy MacNeill had held off failure for one more winter after all.

26

The rain followed us back to New York, slowing us badly, so that it was almost four when we pulled to a stop by a fire hydrant down the block from Frank Donner's apartment building. We had come back by way of the George Washington Bridge, because Donner lived so close to the bridge, and the rain and dimness were such that it had been like driving across a great concrete ribbon between worlds, with nothing but the chasm of space beneath and all around us.

Kerrigan and Rembek and I trotted comically through the rain to Donner's building. None of us had raincoats, because the weather had seemed unthreatening when we'd left New York. We filled the elevator with the rank smell of wet suits. Rembek glared out bullishly from under his brows, spoiling for action, sensing the end but not yet seeing his target.

We had not phoned ahead, and were not expected. Ethel Donner opened the door to us and was instantly gracious and welcoming, taking our wet coats and ushering us into the living room while she went to get Frank.

He was less gracious. He came into the room in undershirt, slippers and old trousers, carrying a hammer; apparently he was doing some home repairs. He said, "Damn it, Ernie, it's Sunday. You know I like to keep my Sundays separate."

"It's my fault," I said. "I wanted to talk to you about that note you wrote."

Everybody looked at me. Ethel Donner, coming in after her husband and feeling the sudden tension in the air, said hesitantly, "Is everything all right? Frank? Is something . . ." It trailed off.

Rembek said, very slowly, "What note? Frank? What note does he mean?"

Donner abruptly shook himself and gave a heavy laugh, saying, "He's out to earn his dough the cheap way, Ernie. I'm just some hood anyway, it don't matter, he'll tie a can on me and take his dough and go home."

Kerrigan said, "Mister Tobin, fill us in. Are you saying Rita didn't write that note?"

"That's what I'm saying."

"Why?"

"It was wrong from the beginning," I said. "The note was written in the wrong style, in the dumb-bunny manner that was her public put-on. If she had really meant to leave Rembek, and wanted to be cruel, the way that real-man business was cruel, she would have chosen a different way. I know her that well now, better than Donner knew her. He saw the public face and thought it was the real her and wrote the note to match."

Kerrigan said, "What would she have done herself, if it was her note?"

"She'd have let him see who she was, now it was too late. She'd have shown him just how bright and complicated and aware she really was, just how little of her he'd ever been allowed to see before."

Rembek said, "I don't like any of this."

Kerrigan said, "Be quiet, Ernie." To me he said, "I think you're right. That would be more her style. So what else have you got?"

"There were three things in life that Rita really cared

about," I said, "and they were money, Ted Quigley, and her acting career. Now she—"

Rembek interrupted violently, shouting, "Quigley! That little sheep? He was out of the picture years ago."

Kerrigan said, "Ernie, argue later if you want. Go on, Mister Tobin. What else?"

I said, "It never seemed in character for Rita Castle to run out that way. The closest thing to a real man in her life was Ted Quigley, and she'd managed to make do on a very small diet of him. And the phrase itself, real man, is something she would never have said in her own voice. And no man at all, not even Quigley, could make her turn her back on financial security and a theatrical career."

Kerrigan said, "You make a good case. All right, what next?"

"If the note's false," I said, "then we've been working from false assumptions all along. We've been looking for the man Rita ran away with, and Rita didn't run away with any man."

Rembek very nearly interrupted again, this time joyously, but controlled himself in time.

I said, "The things we thought were done all by the same person were done by different people. No one took the money away from the motel. If the MacNeills had anything to do with the disappearance of the money, they still didn't murder Rita. Aside from the improbability of their knowing about the money before her death, there's simply insufficient motive for them."

Kerrigan said, "What about the cash? They *could* have found out about it, and they probably needed it."

"They've needed money all their lives," I said. "They never have killed for it and they never will."

"I think you're right," said Kerrigan. "Let's get back to the note. If it's a phony, why was it done? She wasn't dead yet when it was written."

Donner spoke for the first time in a long while, saying, "The frame falls apart there, don't it? You got nothing that makes sense."

"There was a frame, all right," I agreed, "but you're the one who did the framing. You were out to keep Rembek from divorcing your sister and marrying Rita Castle, and you figured the way to do it was discredit Rita, frame her so Rembek wouldn't have any more to do with her."

"Bull," he said.

Kerrigan said to me, "How did he do it?"

"While Rembek was out of town over the weekend," I said, "Donner went to Rita with some sort of story, an emergency of some kind, maybe a tax fraud indictment, I don't know what. He told Rita the story, and told her Rembek was going to have to stay out of New York State for a while, or maybe entirely out of the country. Just for a while. So what she was supposed to do was take the cash from the apartment, go to the motel in Allentown, and wait for Rembek to meet her there. Donner probably told her it might take a week or more before Rembek could show up."

Donner laughed heavily, shaking his head, and said, "Stupid. What's the point? So a week later she comes back and says to Ernie, What's up? Then Ernie's down on me."

Rembek said, "Not if you killed her, Frank."

"It wasn't like that," I said. "If Donner had meant to kill her, he'd just have done it, without complications. But what he wanted was to discredit her, and do it so badly you wouldn't look at Rita Castle or any other woman except your wife for the rest of your life."

Kerrigan said, "So how does he make the frame stick?"

"He finds her," I said. "A week goes by, everybody's

looking for Rita Castle, and all of a sudden Frank Donner finds her. Maybe he fixes it so someone working for him finds her, he smooths that part of it over, and back he comes with Rita in one hand and the cash in the other. He tells Rembek the man got away, and Rembek by that point should be so disgusted with her he won't bother to question the story very much. And when Rita accuses Donner of framing her, all it sounds like is a wild shot aimed at making trouble for the one who found her and dragged her back."

Kerrigan, looking at Rembek, studying him, said, "It might have worked, too. Yes, it probably would have worked. You've got a big temper, Ernie, you would have blown up and never listened to Rita at all."

Rembek said, belligerently, "I would have listened. I would have known it was a frame. For Christ's sake, you think I'm that easy to sucker?"

"Frank Donner did," I said. "And I'm inclined to agree with him."

Donner said, "How come it's me? Why not anybody else? Just because I'm Eleanor's brother?"

"You did a stretch for forgery once," I reminded him. "You're the best bet to have written the note. You were also up for arson once or twice, which connects with the explosion in my office, which we haven't gotten to yet."

"Let's get to it," said Kerrigan.

"That's easy," I said. "What he wanted to do was destroy the note. It was a safe forgery when it was simply a part of a frame-up, but when it was a piece of evidence in a murder it was too chancy to leave around. So he snuck into the office to get it. Stealing it would have pointed a finger at it, so he figured to destroy it in the explosion. I don't know why he had to make it a booby trap, and turn it into a killing, but he did."

Donner said, "This is a great fairy story, but let's see the footprints under the window."

I told him, "I don't know if you bothered to bribe the doorman at Rita Castle's apartment building or not, but even if you did, it was a bribe that could only hold up as part of the frame. It won't hold up now. It may take a few minutes, but Rembek can get that doorman to tell at what point that weekend you went into the building to leave the note."

Rembek said, "I'll make a phone call right now."

I said, "Is it necessary, Donner?"

He wouldn't give an inch. He said, "Ernie, if you listen to this bullshit, I'll remember it. The phone's right over there. If you believe this hard-on cop over me, go ahead and use it."

Rembek didn't hesitate. He went over and made his call. When he was done, he turned back to us and said, "They'll call as soon as they get it."

Kerrigan said, "Mister Tobin, you're answering all the questions but the big one. We know about the money, we know about the note, we know about the explosion. What about who killed Rita?"

"That's for Donner to answer," I said. "He was the only one who knew where she was. I can't think of any reason he'd change his plans and kill her himself, though it's vaguely possible. I think it more likely he told someone else where she was, and that someone else went and killed her."

Kerrigan shook his head. "I don't like that," he said. "Why would he tell anybody?"

Rembek said, "He killed her himself, the bastard. He knew the frame wouldn't work, and he killed her himself."

I said, "Who did you tell, Donner?"

"Me," said a woman, stepping through the doorway.

We all turned and looked at her, and before Rembek said, hoarsely, "Eleanor!" I knew who it had to be.

She was a thin woman, bird-thin, as painfully thin as Ethel

Donner was painfully fat. Her black dress, with a narrow belt at the waist, hung loosely on her, as though she'd suffered a recent weight loss. Her hair was black, heavily mixed with gray, and piled without neatness atop her head.

It was her eyes that told who she was; black bright, intense, with the stare of a hawk but behind the brightness was a fog of pain and confusion. I remembered eyes like that from my early days on the force, when I was on a beat. I'd seen men and women like this before, the chronic asylum-dwellers, the people who spend their adult lives in and out of mental hospitals, who function nominally for periods of time and then— abruptly or slowly—go off again on a high wailing curve to some far mountaintop the sane can never reach. I remember being called upon from time to time when one of these people had suddenly reached the stage where the hospital was necessary again. Sometimes they would be huddling in a corner of the bed, sometimes sitting docile and quiet in the living room with their bags packed by their feet, sometimes hiding in a dark closet with their bright eyes peering out at a world too complex to be borne.

I had thought it would be her, but never having met her I couldn't be sure. I had wanted Frank Donner to mention her first, but this was even better. She had come out to us herself.

I said, "Good afternoon, Mrs. Rembek. I'm sorry to have to meet you this way."

"It's gone on long enough," she said. "We might as well end it now." She made a thin apologetic smile for her brother, saying, "I'm sorry, Frank, but it is all over."

I said, "You overheard Frank and his wife talking about it, didn't you?"

"I listen," she said. "Nobody knows, but I do. I know everything that happens. I heard Ethel tell you about the snoring, I heard everything."

She was, at the moment, being absolutely rational, with only the faintest hint of wild winds in her voice. Still, I felt the tremendous pressure she was under, the strain of her control on herself. I said, "You don't have to talk about it now if you don't want, Mrs. Rembek."

But she wanted to. She said, "Ernie thinks he hides things from me, but he never could. I've heard him talking on the telephone with his women, I heard him talking to Sam Goldberg about a divorce."

"That's impossible!" shouted Rembek, in a kind of horror.

"Sit down, Ernie," said Kerrigan, and for the first time the full cold weight of the corporation could be heard glinting in his voice. "Sit down and shut up."

I said, "Mrs. Rembek, excuse me. Is that why you came to stay here, at your brother's? Because you knew about the divorce proceedings?"

"I couldn't stay there any longer," she said, faint remembered panic in her voice. "Pretending, pretending, making believe I was deaf and blind, I couldn't do it any more." She looked suddenly around the room, back and forth, like a trapped animal, but all she said was, "I would like to sit down, please."

Kerrigan and Frank Donner both hurried forward with chairs; with an apologetic thank-you smile to Kerrigan she chose the one brought by her brother, who hovered over her as she gingerly settled down. Continuing to stand beside her, Donner then turned to glare at me, saying, "You can't use any of this stuff and you know it. She isn't responsible." He looked vaguely comic in his undershirt, the hammer still held forgotten in his right hand, his face and neck red with rage and frustration and confusion.

His sister took his other hand, saying, "Please, Frank, let me talk. It's really all right."

194

And all at once I was sick of it. At the end of all the lies, all
the false trails, the bloodshed and violence and intrigue, was a
beaten and lonely woman. Of everyone I had met in the
course of the hunt, this woman was the least criminal, the
most to be pitied, the least to be feared, and yet she was the
prey I'd been tracking.

"No more," I said. "No more, Mrs. Rembek. Tell your
story to the police, if you want, I can't have it." Turning to
Rembek, I gestured at his wife and said, "There she is. You
sent me to find her, and I found her. Do what you think you
should do with her."

I considered adding something more, telling him a bit of
the truth about Rita Castle, some of the things Ted Quigley
had told me, but I left them unsaid. Rembek was staring with
glazed eyes at his wife, seeing her for what must have been the
first time; to learn the truth about both the women in his life
at once would have been too brutal.

I went over to the telephone, picked it up, and started dialing. Donner shouted at me, "Who do you think you're
calling?"

"The police," I said, turning to look at him.

"You can't touch Eleanor," he said angrily, "she isn't responsible, the whole thing's something she made up in her
head!"

"It isn't for Eleanor," I said, "it's for you. There's the
Mickey Hansel killing, that one's yours. And you *are* responsible, and it will stick."

The dam burst. Donner's hand came up with the hammer
in it, his face reddened, and with a roar he lunged across the
room at me.

I acted without conscious thought. My hand dropped the
phone and reached back, flipping the tail of my jacket clear,
closing on the butt of the revolver, bringing it out as I leaned

to the left, all the movements I'd learned years ago on the pistol range and done so often they were now mechanical. The gun came out, Donner rushed toward me with the hammer swinging in his hand, and I shot him twice in the head.

27

The next two days were full of questions. My testimony was taken several times, by both tape recorder and stenographer.

The others were asked questions, too; Rembek and his wife and Mrs. Donner. Kerrigan had asked to be allowed to fade out of the picture before I called the police, and I saw no reason to refuse him.

Talk is an antidote to pain, so though Rembek (who was not charged with anything) would do no talking at all, both women were more than willing to explain what had happened and why. I had been right about Donner's motive and method in getting Rita Castle to take Rembek's money and hide out in Pennsylvania. Mrs. Rembek insisted that she had gone to see Rita Castle—having overheard in a conversation between the Donners where Rita was—not to kill her but only to talk with her, in hopes of getting Rita to promise to keep away from Rembek in the future. She'd brought along a pistol of her brother's, with which she hoped to frighten Rita, but the pistol hadn't been loaded. However, Rita wouldn't scare, and Mrs. Rembek made a slip that told her of the frame that had been set up. After that, Rita was apparently deliberately cruel; she had just finished a shower, and now she stepped out of her robe and, in Mrs. Rembek's words, "paraded herself around to show me the difference between us." That was when Mrs. Rembek clubbed her with the butt of the pistol, all her pent-up feelings coming out in one violent lethal blow.

197

Later, on the way back to New York she'd thrown the pistol and room key from the Easton-Phillipsburg bridge into the Delaware River.

The two women differed on one point, Mrs. Rembek insisting that no one had learned what she'd done, Mrs. Donner insisting she for one had known it all along. Whether or not Frank Donner himself had been aware of the truth, there was no way to be sure, though he had probably at least suspected it.

As to the killing of Mickey Hansel, Mrs. Donner maintained that it had not originally been intended to happen. Her husband had heard from Kerrigan in the course of our first interview about my office and my penchant for filing things, and had assumed that's where he would find the note. He'd gone there at four in the morning, gotten in past the nightman, who was asleep, jimmied the lock and prepared to create a fire that would destroy all the papers—in fact, all the furniture—in the office. While he was setting things up, Mickey Hansel came creeping in. Donner collared him, and Hansel admitted he'd come up to steal the typewriter for pawning to get something to drink. Hansel also told him he was supposed to be present at nine in the morning, and I was to come in later. At this point it was impossible for Donner to let Hansel live, since Hansel would have told me about Donner's presence in the office, so Donner strangled him, set a time bomb in the filing cabinet, propped Hansel's body against an open file drawer, and went away. When the explosion went off at 9:05 in the morning, we all assumed Hansel had just arrived and been killed by a bomb with some sort of triggering device.

Indirect corroboration of this story came from the elevator man at that building, who didn't remember taking Mickey Hansel up to the office Saturday morning.

As to me, it looked for a while as though I might be in some trouble myself. No one questioned the fact that I had killed Frank Donner in self-defense, but there was a great deal of official displeasure at my having done so with a gun for which I had no permit. There was also official displeasure at my having braced Donner and Mrs. Rembek with the truth before reporting my findings to the authorities. But in the end a certain pragmatic attitude on the part of the force saved me from anything worse than a couple of tough lectures. It was generally conceded I'd done the job, cracking a case from the inside that would have been just about impossible to crack from the outside, and nothing excuses like success.

Not that anyone was in a hurry to reinstate me. I was still a bad odor at Centre Street, and always would be. The most they were willing to do was forgive me a few irregularities.

Through all of this Marty Kengelberg was very helpful, standing up for me, cutting through channels to see people on my behalf, and giving me interim pep talks when I wasn't giving testimony elsewhere. It was ungracious of me to remember some of the angry things he'd said to me at the house, but I couldn't help myself. I hope I managed successfully to cover my feelings; he deserves that much.

By Wednesday, it was all over. Kate and Bill had come back from Patchogue on Sunday night, of course, but the household wasn't back to normal until Wednesday, when I was no longer required to go into Manhattan and answer questions.

The rain had continued all through Monday, but Tuesday was clearing and Wednesday dawned with a great golden sun. I went back to my wall for the first time in days, digging a portion, laying the concrete block as I went, absorbing my attention in the details of the task at hand. I did no more thinking about the murder of Rita Castle.

199

Nine days later, on a Friday, Kate came out to the yard with an envelope that had just come in the mail. Inside it were two checks from Continental Projects, Incorporated, one for five thousand dollars, marked "For professional services," and the other for three hundred dollars, marked "Miscellaneous expenses."

I said, "Good. That'll carry us quite a while. I'll endorse them when I come in for lunch."

She said, "Mitch, didn't it change anything?"

I looked at her. "Change what?"

"All right," she said. "Lunch in about an hour."

She went into the house, and I went back to my wall.